To: Bc

The D'Angelo

Cursed

Spirit

TALES OF CHARLES ISLAND
TALE 1

Marissa D'Angelo

Dedication

This book is dedicated to my grandparents and teachers

who sparked my fascination of storytelling.

Author's Note

Since the release of this book, I have wanted to find some way to help Charles Island and the wildlife that it supports. A local reforestation group is working hand in hand with the Connecticut Department of Energy and Environmental Protection to plant more trees so that the island and its wildlife can survive and thrive.

Message from Reforestation Group:

We want to restore the island to its former state. After years of invasive species and diseases, we need to help nature along with this task.

10% of the proceeds from this series will go to this cause.

Catori

1

The brisk emptiness of winter enveloped the land in a
white silence. Breaths exhaled formed smoky ghosts
within the dry air. Most living had ventured south long
before although some braved the harsh season. Each
lone branch on the trees reached up for any sliver of
warmth they could receive from the sun. They stood
tall, but bare.

The Natives respected this land of theirs. For after
the dreaded winter would come many fruits to feast on.
It was a climate that took years and years of adjustment.
Animals were their sole reason for survival as they used

their furs for warmth and nutrients for food. Catori lay beneath some of the furs and poked his head out.

"Ka'," short for mom in their tribal language. "Where is dad?" Mom paced around, carrying dried salmon that had been stored previously. Her long, dark hair hung down just past her waist and swayed as she walked around.

"Hunting for deer," she said. He squeezed his eyes shut as hard as he could, frustrated with himself for not waking up in time. He was supposed to learn the ways of his father so he could take care of their village. After all, he was next in line as chief of their tribe. Catori was the only child that the chief had which made everyone extra careful about sending him out with the others. This only upset him more because it made him feel like a child although he had been alive for seventeen winters.

He decided to go anyway despite how warm the bed was, he jumped out of it and peered underneath to grab day clothes. There was a light brown tunic rested on top of the pile. His mother had made it from a hunt that father went on last year. As he placed it over his head, he could feel someone's eyes on him. Mom was right in front of him with her hands on her hips.

"And what do you think you're doing?" She asked. He got up anyway and started towards the door.

"I'm going to go help Pa," she took the tunic off the shelf before he could get it.

"You don't know where he is. Take the pole, Catori. Maybe there will be some fish." She stepped in front of him and touched his forehead gently.

"I know you want to make your father proud. And you do. Every day. He'll be happy enough with some fish."

He sighed, but agreed. Mom still thought of him as a toddler at times. She pushed the tunic over his head and kissed him on the cheek before sending him off to fish.

Outside was painfully beautiful. The snow from yesterday softened nature's grounds. He took regretful footsteps, ruining the soft surface. With each step, he felt the snow pack down beneath him. It was slightly warmer today so the trees let off the heavy snow that had been weighing their branches down. A nearby stream that led into the ocean was a few trees away. Unlike any other season, there was a dead silence. On a nice spring day, you could hear the birds chirp and fly out from their nests in the full trees. There were still some, but the only sound made were his steps.

When the stream appeared ahead, it was narrow which meant most of its waters were back in the ocean at low tide. The great spirit caused low and high tides. When they were low in the summer, many shells would wash ashore and that meant the spirits were pleased with his tribe. However, when the tides were high, it would take all of those gifts away - teaching his tribe strength and persistence.

In the winter, it was a different story. Higher tides allowed Catori to not have to travel as far in order to fish. Catori came at the wrong time. He continued on anyway as he promised his mom a fish so if he had to, he would venture out further towards the shore.

As he reached the coast, rocks poked out of the snow. They created a path that led to a smaller island. The low tide had revealed a path that he could follow, which was almost too perfect. He paused for a moment and looked out as he said a prayer privately to himself.

Sacred Land, Poquahaug, you have been with my ancestors for many, many winters. The food and land you give us is sacred. We give back each day as a thank you.

Catori was named after his father saw a spirit of their ancestors from this land. The spirit had warned him not to travel across the pathway since high tide was coming. His life had been saved by that spirit. When his father returned, his mother broke the news of her pregnancy and they were quick to name him spirit in their tribal language: Catori.

Sacred Land

2

As soon as the island came into view, Catori noticed how bare and small it appeared. The desolate trees towered over the land. He had only been there a few times, but it was mostly used as a spiritual place for his tribe. People walk up to the edge of the coast to pray to their ancestors, but they would never travel down the path and step foot on the island itself. Waves sent bubbling white foam over the sandy shores and retreated back to reveal rock-covered soil all along the coast. Moisture from the water cleared some of the snow that had already melted a bit. He winced at the sight of the rocks, remembering how they cut up his bare feet when he would come here as a child and didn't know any better.

Catori rested his supplies against a colossal boulder and decided to lean back on it to look out at the island. The sun's light reflected in the waters that lay between him and the unexplored land. Its warmth felt better than being in the shade of the woods. He closed his eyes and let his mind take him elsewhere — to the first time he was brought here.

"Don't get too close," Pa said putting his muscular arm out in front of him. His hair was just as long as his mother's was now. It went down to his waist, but he always kept it back by tying it with a long, thin piece of deer hide. Despite his rugged features and dark hair, soft brown eyes stood out and you could feel the passion from within him.

Catori looked up at his father because back then, he came nowhere close to being as tall as he was. He had to have only seen six or seven winters at the time.

He reached his arms out towards the island. Even then, it called out to him and he felt it deep in his chest that he was meant to go there. His curiosity tempted him to wander towards it many times. Pa repeated himself, sterner this time.

"No, this is sacred land. Sit down." He quickly obeyed his father's orders and sat on a larger rock that was part of a circle that they would hold meetings at with their tribe. There were similar sized rocks that had flat surfaces to sit on. A very long time ago, when his ancestors set foot on the land... there had been great disagreement between them and neighboring tribes. Originally, they would stand in a circle to come together so that they could reach some type of common ground. After a while of indecision and arguments, the

Paugussetts claimed this territory. Our ancestors continued holding meetings with their own people so much so that they carried rocks over and formed a circle signifying togetherness and eternal tradition.

He and his father were the first two to come to the meeting because his father led it, being the chief. Whispers and footsteps echoed around him as he seemed to find their source and saw several friends his age coming out of the trees with their fathers. The women stayed back to create a feast that they would all eat when they came back. One friend who was much taller and stockier than Catori but around the same age, walked right over to him and waved.

"Ready for the meeting, Mato?" Catori asked.

"Sure am, what will we learn this time?" He asked, curious. Mato translated to Bear. Although Mato's father's name was different, people oftentimes called him that for his stocky, bear-like features as a nickname, which he then named his son. It was fitting because even as a young kid, Mato had broader shoulders than the rest of the boys and his dark brown hair was shagged and resembled a bear's fur as his family kept it shorter than the rest of the boys.

"I do not know, but I have a feeling it will be about the forbidden island." Catori looked down.

"Alright, I brought this to practice my song for later on," Mato pulled out a hollow, wooden tool with a few holes on the top. He put it away and walked back over to his father. As soon as they took their seats around the circle, Pa went in the center and began speaking.

"We have come here today to teach our young about the sacred land. If you look out towards the moon, you will see its reflection cast a shadow on the island. This is a sacred land where our ancestors stay to keep us safe. We do not go there often. In fact, this is a place that we can worship from the shores as we do not want to disrupt our ancestors. Every so often, there will be a path that leads you to the island...this is a test. A test of temptation and self-control. In order to pass this test, one must respect the land and worship from afar." He paused and gave Catori a look as if he specifically said the last part for him.

Pa joined the circle by sitting on the rock beside Catori and closed his eyes. Catori looked around at everyone and noticed that they followed suit by closing their eyes, too. He closed his for a moment and listened closely to the waves crashing against the sand and rocks. A ringing came in his ears, causing him to quickly open his eyes. He looked around. All others seemed to be in a trance; their eyes still shut and bodies frozen. Catori peered out at the island and could see the moon's reflection in the water beside it. There wasn't a cloud in the sky - the stars illuminated the land around them as well. Another distinct glow came from the island itself. At first, it was a flaming light and he was almost concerned *that the island was on fire. After blinking a few times, he saw the light contained in one single spot of the island - the entrance of which the rock path led up to the mainland. The glow became more recognizable to him as the outline of an owl. When his grandmother told him stories before bedtime, she was incredibly fond of including an owl in each one. They symbolized truth and curiosity. Catori wished to be that owl since he likely knew the truths of the island and could soar above ensuring safety all while continuing to give into his curiosity. Just when he was about to get his father's attention, it spread its illuminated wings and flew off towards the back of the island; out of his sight.*

"Hey, what are you doing?" Someone called out, snapping Catori out of his flashback. He jumped where he stood, knocking over the fishing pole and supplies that he had carefully rested against the boulder.

Aponi

3

One of his friends from the village walked over to him and started to pick up his supplies that had fallen over. If it was one of the other men in the tribe, they would surely report on the meager amount of fish that Catori was able to catch which was none.

"Aponi," he said, taking a deep breath in. He was relieved to see her because unlike the other men, she wouldn't tell anyone that he was unsuccessful in his attempt at earning his standing. Aponi had grown up with him. Both of their parents raised them close by since they were born in the same season, too. She came up just below his shoulder and wore her hair back in two braids. Deep raven-colored strands blew in the breeze, emanating the unforgettable lavender in which she would always soak. When she walked over, the sun caused her chestnut brown eyes to glisten all the more. Painted tribal designs made of raspberries and roots trailed down her arms all the way to her fingertips. Today, they were concealed by a heavy fur covering much like his own. She had deerskin boots lined with fur that went up to her knees. Masking the boots that hugged close to her legs was a deer hide dress with countless fringes that hung down, stopping just before her toes. The embroidered dress resembled their tribe with various colors that were plants and other harvested items native to their territory. Catori had to think for a moment on why he had come down here in the first place.

"Fishing," he said, simply. "You?" They both knew all too well that he had come here for more than just that.

She would find him here quite often, looking out at the land that he was not allowed to venture out to. Sometimes, his family would ask her where he was and never once did she reveal his secret. If his father... the chief... knew that he was making frequent visits to the coastline just to stare out at the island, he would surely put an end to it in fear of the danger that could come Catori's way. It made him all the more curious.

"Your mom sent me to get you," she smiled. "And I thought.. 'hm...where else could he be?" She playfully pushed him on the chest, sending him back against the boulder. Despite the frigid air, the warmth of her touch sent his body into a tingling sensation. He felt himself wanting more, but he knew that they were just friends – although it was difficult to ignore the feeling that would rise in him at times. Before he could protest, she had already grabbed several of his supplies and headed back towards their village.

He picked up the remaining items and ran after her. "Hey, I can't go back without any fish!"

"Do you know how long you've been out here?" She asked. He stayed silent but looked out at the sun that was just going down. "Guess not. There's a reason your mother sent me looking for you..." she must have noticed that he wasn't following any longer because he refused to go back without at least one fish. He might as well go live in solidarity instead of comeback as the chief's son unable to benefit his tribe in any way.

After reaching a few trees' distance from Catori, she glanced back at him and shrugged,

"Okay... let's get you a fish," as she turned back in the other direction and led him towards the shore. This time, she went the opposite direction that he had originally gone. Although Aponi was in on Catori's unending curiosity, there was something that only Catori had known about her as well. Instead of harvesting with the other women in the tribe, she would often wander off herself... when they were just children, Catori promised to teach her how to fish and hunt. These were not typical things for women to do in a tribe, but she persisted so much to the point that Catori gave in and didn't think much of it. After a few lessons, Aponi's strength and resilience showed. When he would try to use his bow and arrow to hunt something small such as a rabbit, it would be Aponi that landed her arrow first. Fishing went just about the same way.

They reached the shore again, except this was a less rocky path that she had chosen. Taking the long, wooden stick that he had just held, she carefully walked with its tip facing down. At the very end of it was a rock that had been chiseled down. This blade was ideal for standing in the shallow waters and waiting for the calm until fish would dart by. Catori watched in admiration as he saw Aponi's agile strategy of climbing atop a few rocks so that she did not have to wade in the water which would then disturb the fish. She pressed the front of her body down onto the rock that was as long as two of her then peered down at the adjacent waters. In a few moments, she drew the spear back and sent it forward in a deliberate, precise manner. Catori walked over but stayed a bit away as not to scare the fish. Just when he came next to her, she pulled the spear up and out of the water again revealing a fish at the end, spear through its twitching body.

"Can I give you credit this time?" Catori said as he held out a bowl to place the fish in. She shook her head right away as that would mean letting the others know about her secret. If she was going to keep Catori's secret safe, then he had to as well. All the same, he felt guilty for taking the credit on something that he did not do. She ignored his request and continued walking back to their tribe.

"Did you see anything this time on the island?" She changed the subject. Aponi was fully aware of what happened that night many years before when he saw the glowing owl. When he first told her, she didn't believe him. But after more and more spiritual talks from the elders, she grew more and more curious.

"No, not this time. I want to go out there," he couldn't believe he said that aloud given how much trouble he would be in if it got out that he was thinking of venturing out.

"You know you can't do that," she said. "You would fail the test."

"But what if that's not what the ancestors meant to happen? What if the test is just something that we made up as a misunderstanding of their wishes?" He pondered the thought that had been circling his mind for a while now. Aponi didn't respond as if it sent her mind into deep, complex thought too.

"We need to listen to our elders. That is the safest way. But you are right, there is a possibility that could be true too..." she said.

Their conversation felt like it lasted a while because as soon as they grew silent, they had made it back to their home. His father should be back from hunting by now and all would feast together in the long house, wigwam. Aponi handed Catori his supplies and smirked at him.

"I'll see you at dinner, okay? No more bright ideas about venturing out there - not without me, anyway. Oh, and nice catch by the way," she winked at him and walked off. Did this mean that she was open to going with him to the island even though it was against their tribes' wishes?

Harvest

4

The ground was still slightly covered in snow and anything that melted would freeze overnight since the sun was already setting. It cast its rays through the openings between each tree causing them to maintain dimming shadows over the land. Catori walked up to his home so that he could put his supplies away, hoping that his mother was already in the long house so she wouldn't ask him questions about why he had been out for so long. She would ask him about what he was doing instead… was he okay… he shouldn't go off by himself anymore… these questions, although coming from her heart, made him feel belittled and as if he was no better than a child. He was trying to gain some honor from others and become stronger for the tribe's sake. His own curiosity seemed to have a way of winning him over, though.

He stepped in and to his surprise, mother was not there so he put away the supplies quickly and headed back out for the long house. He would see Aponi there too. Catori was grateful for her as he knew she would keep his secret safe. Growing up, the other men had joked around and said that they were in love, but they had always just been friends.

Their home was the closest to the long house being that his father was chief. Even though they were the closest, it still took him a little while to get there - being more inland. All of the others' homes were close together, but in all surrounded the longhouse, modeled after the circle that they would meet at on the shore. He couldn't see anyone else walking there, which meant that he was late... per the usual. Some chief in training he was... A thick deerskin rested over the opening of the house, concealing all that was inside. He brushed it aside and entered. Everyone sat in a circle on the ground and were waiting for him to start their prayer before they began their feast. It was difficult to gather food in the winter since animals and fish were scarce. Many did not make it through winter because of this. They would all work together towards gathering and hunting then share what they found with the group. This helped to ensure everyone had a chance at survival through the winter.

As soon as he walked in, he took place beside his father and mother who left a spot open for him. He knelt down, continuing to look around the circle. He saw his grandmother that knelt by his father. She closely resembled him with the long, thick hair, except many shades of gray hung down and her hair was quite disheveled all of the time. Freckles covered the entirety of her face and her skin was a deep brown, it had a contagious warmth to it. The kind that made you want to stay even longer in her presence. Unlike father, her eyes were a darker shade of brown and said to have been passed down to Catori. Looking into them felt like looking at his own soul in a way.

Then, there was Aponi and her parents. Aponi caught sight of him glancing around and squeezed her eyes shut at him, signaling him to do the same. He followed. She was a rule follower and it could get a little annoying at times, but he knew that she was just trying to help him so he didn't get in trouble.

They sat there together for what seemed like forever. Pieces of lavender that had been harvested over the summer filled the air with a calming aroma. It could put you to sleep if you stayed there long enough. They sat in silence so that they could say private prayers to their ancestors and nature. If it wasn't for the sacrifices of nature, they would not have food to keep them alive. He felt his father get up beside him and that's when he knew it was time to open his eyes again.

"Thank you for all of your support, we wouldn't be able to do this without you. Let's feast," his father said in the middle of their circle. He got up and headed right towards his dad as everyone else formed a line to gather food in their wooden bowls.

"Hey, missed you this morning," Catori shyly said. He always grew timid when it came time to talk to him. He was just so much more than Catori ever dreamed to be so he set the bar pretty high for him. His father passed him a bowl and they joined the line of people.

"We get up with the sun and hunt. Let's try again tomorrow, ok?" He bluntly said as they moved through the line. He plopped a thick piece of venison onto his plate then Catori's. The bowl nearly fell out of his hands as he wasn't expecting so much weight to pile on so suddenly. Moving on, there was a large bowl of clams that had been dried for winter's use. He took two of them and placed them in his bowl next to the venison. As they neared the end of the line, his father walked off in a different direction and Catori realized that his mom had been right behind him the whole time in line.

She followed him over to sit down. "Don't be so hard on yourself. He's tough, but only because he sets the stakes high so that you can be ready in case your people need you as they need him right now. It's a big responsibility, but don't forget that he loves you." She reassured him. Catori nodded in agreement although part of him just still didn't feel good enough. When they sat back down, he started chewing on his venison. Its rich, earthy texture sent his mouth into a satisfying heaven. He wished that he could grab more but knew

that this was the tribe's most difficult season.
Grandmother walked over and joined them.

"Hey, you guys trying to lose me back there? I saw you for one minute then you vanished," she joked around about how slow she was, but she wasn't at all.

"No, grandma. What did you do today?" He asked. At this point, his mother got up and ventured off to talk to some of the other women.

"Oh you see…I went off to the island and walked around a bit, talked to my husband…" she said.

"Come on, grandma! You can't be serious," he said. It was funny how she didn't seem to care about the rules at all.

"No, no…I just washed some clothes, but what were you up to, hmm? I heard you and Aponi got together," she was dying for them to 'admit their feelings for one another.' In fact, she would even set them up at times thinking everything would finally fall into place. Catori questioned if it was grandma that had suggested Aponi

go looking for him earlier. It probably was. Grandma's

wish couldn't happen if the feelings weren't mutual,

though. Catori was sure that Aponi did not take interest

in him. There were many other men in the tribe who

actually woke up early to go hunting and would be a

much better match for her.

"Are you the one who sent her after me when I was

fishing?" He asked.

"Well, who else was going to help you actually bring

a fish back?" she whispered. His face must have given

away his embarrassment because he could feel his

cheeks grow flush and the sweat from his palms almost

made him drop his bowl on the ground.

"You know how it is, grandma. I get lost looking out

at the island. Why can't we go there?" He asked. She

didn't answer at first and just looked around ensuring

that no one was listening or close by.

"The island is only meant for spirits and our ancestors. We don't go there because it is not safe. Not all spirits are good, you know," she answered. And with that, Catori's curiosity grew even more.

A Day's Hunt

5

The night after the feast was a complete struggle for Catori to fall asleep. He could hear his father's snores and mother's shallow breaths. He just lay there, tossing and turning in his bed. Mind wandering from one place to the next... Before he knew it, the sun was creeping up from the horizons and let light in through the cracks of the door. When the snoring stopped, he knew his father was already up and getting ready to go so Catori decided to get up too even though he felt like he had no energy. His dad came out of the other room and seemed surprised to see him up.

"I'm coming today," Catori said. Dad nodded. They both finished getting ready and dressing accordingly with their deer tunics and fur coverings on along with long boots then headed out into the woods.

As soon as they stepped outside, Catori immediately regretted not coming out this early more often. There was a peaceful beauty that echoed from the generous amount of sunlight that trickled in. It seemed even more bright than ever, being that the trees were bare and unable to block out its rays. Pa had gone behind their home for a few moments, but came back with two bowstrings and a long, but narrow shoulder bag that contained a bundle of arrows. Catori grabbed one of the bowstrings and offered to take the bag, but his father persisted on carrying it around his shoulder. They continued on, away from their village. Passing by some of the other homes, Catori kept his gaze on Aponi's – waiting to see if she would come out. It was unlikely that she would since harvesting did not have to happen until a bit later in the day. The morning was meant for prayers to their ancestors' spirits. As they went deeper within the forest and their tribe's homes disappeared from their view, the dwellings of various animals surrounded them. As some of the animals were unheard from during this time, they slept through until the flowers began to bloom again and grasses poked through the earth's soft grounds. If people could learn how to sleep through the winter too, they would not have to worry about so many of their tribespeople not surviving. Tall, bare branches blocked out a modest amount of sunlight unlike the summers. They traveled farther from the coast since father liked to hunt more inland, his excuse being that the bulkier game was in that direction.

"Did you sleep at all last night?" He broke the silence as he looked over at his son, continuing to walk further.

"Not a wink," Catori answered.

"You need your sleep to hunt, but I guess this is good training for the future. We need to practice under such conditions just in case," he assured him. Catori was hoping that this would be a one time thing where he hunted on no sleep, but his father seemed to like the idea...

"So what kept you up, huh? Thinking about that fish you caught that took you the whole day?" He teased him. Catori pushed him playfully to the side.

"Oh come on, time got away from me. That's all. Mom sent Aponi after me...or I think grandma did, I'm not sure." He said. He was quick to change the subject from her because he knew his dad felt exactly how his grandmother and mom felt. "I lost track of daylight. I was looking out at the island and thinking of the stories that you used to tell everyone. Have you ever been out there?"

"You know what is expected, Catori." His tone was now stern and serious.

"I know we're not allowed to go, but was just wondering if you've gone before the rule?" Catori pressed on.

Pa sighed, "You know, it was when we were young that we were able to go out there. Our elders warned us of the possible dangers, but our curiosity won us over. At first, it was nice but then we saw exactly what they were talking about. So we got together and agreed to make it a rule for our people." He stopped in his tracks and his son noticed the sudden shift. His tone was no longer stern. Instead, it was full of sorrow and mourning. "Some of us have lost so much to the island. We do not want any more loss than we've already had."

Before Catori could ask his father anymore questions, he put out his arm, signaling him to stop moving and placed his index finger over his mouth. Pa crept forward with slow, quiet steps as his son watched, admiringly. In just a few moments, a buck walked out from behind one of the thickest trees in the forest. He didn't seem to see them so he continued on. Pa passed an arrow over to Catori and at first, he shook his head insisting his father take the shot. He wasn't taking no for an answer, though.

Catori had never made as big of a kill before and now he surely had to or then he would definitely be considered a failure by his dad. He had pretty good aim from practicing on pretend targets, but he felt that didn't prepare him enough for the real thing. The buck's short fur blended with the tree bark that it stood against. If not for its movements, they would not have been able to point it out. White circles surrounded its black eyes. A patch of white was just under its mouth and the inside of its legs. Muscular legs proved how fast he would run if startled. It didn't notice them yet and continued walking. Catori was taught from a young age how important nature was to the tribe and their very existence. Many times, he missed his target purposely because he felt that they should continue to live their life just as he was able to live his.

He took the arrow out of his hand and set it into his bow, pushing it back against the string and aiming it a little bit ahead of the buck. He wanted it to walk right into his targeted spot. This all-required patience and self-control. Everything around the buck was blocked from existence. He knew he had to get this for his tribe so that they could continue through the winter. This would last them for a while. What stood out even more to him was getting this buck to prove to his father that he could be the man that he wanted him to be although he knew he wasn't.

Catori noticed its wide antlers and wondered how it could carry so much weight on its head. It led its pack and ensured a safe route for them from day to day. He squeezed his eyes shut and as soon as he opened them up again, pulled back his arrow at full force. It went up and through the air. The buck took a quick look his way and seemed to stare right into his eyes. He felt the gaze strike him deep in his core. Both of its ears were up and alert for the moment until the arrow went straight through its chest, sending him over on his side. A doe and fawn went running in the opposite direction as fast as they could to get away. The father sacrificed himself for his family.

His dad ran over to the buck and put him out of his misery as he took his last breath. Catori knelt beside him. He knew what would come next. He had just taken something from the earth and it was only right to pray for this, showing their appreciation. He looked over at Pa and he was deep in meditation, but Catori could not seem to concentrate in the slightest. His mind kept playing the doe and fawn over and over again as they fled in desperation, unable to even say goodbye. He caused that.

When his father opened his eyes, he instructed him to get the back of the buck while he would get the front and they would bring him back to their village.

Regret

6

When they made it back to the village, Catori couldn't bear to watch this buck get torn apart even more.

"Hey Pa, do you think you and the guys can finish the rest? I told grandma that I would help her," was the only excuse he could think of at the time. It was true though. Yesterday, grandma had asked if he could come meet her because she had to show him something. They both let go of the buck so that it slid back onto the ground.

"Sure, nice job today! I am so proud of you," he said. This was one of the rare occasions that he saw his father smile from ear to ear. "Who knew that no sleep could be even better at bringing you luck?"

He couldn't have been more wrong. He just nodded at his father and turned to walk towards his home. His grandmother lived with them in the same smaller wigwam. This was the custom for each family; all generations would live together and stay close. He moved the deerskin that was draped over the doorway so he could enter, but only found his mother folding things and cleaning up.

"Where's grandma," he asked. She jumped as if she wasn't expecting him for a while longer.

"Oh, Catori! You scared me. Did you guys get anything out there today? You're back early," she noted.

"It was fine. Do you know where grandma is?" He tried his best to stop any other questions from being asked. It was a difficult thing to do with his mother though. This time, she didn't persist. Catori didn't want to tell her although she would find out soon enough. When he should have felt more proud than ever, he didn't because he took something away from someone else. He wondered how the deer family would survive without the buck to keep them safe.

"She's out back near the pond. She said she would wash some of our clothes and hang them inside when she is finished," she turned back to what she had been doing before.

"Ok thanks, be right back."

Just as his mother said, grandma was by the pond. She was kneeling down, pushing various pieces of deerskin into the water and rubbing them with a mix of fragrances that had been dried and stored from the warmer season. In their village, she was one of the most knowledgeable when it came to lavender, jade and other fragrances.

"You killed an animal, huh?" Grandma muttered under her breath without turning back. He didn't even expect her to know that he was standing there.

"Did the news travel that quickly?" He asked, kneeling beside her and taking the deerskin in his hand to continue her work for her. She handed him the lavender to press into it.

"You feel bad," reading his mind. He didn't expect any less from her.

"The buck was huge and will help our people survive through the winter. But he had a family of his own and I took that away from them," he paused. "I saw his young as they watched their father get taken right before their eyes." He could feel a tear stream down his cheek and wiped it right away. This was no way for the chief's son to be acting.

"It is a good thing for you to feel this way. Do not be ashamed. This means that you are more connected with the earth and its animals as if they are one of your own. The others may spend their entire lives getting to that point, but you are already there," grandma took the clothes from him and started squeezing them out. She set them across several rocks to dry in the sun.

"I want to go back and make another decision, but it is too late now. I need to become used to this because it will be an everyday thing for me as the chief's son," he said, seeking any advice at all that she could give.

"That is your problem right there. You refer to yourself as 'Chief's son.' That is no way to define oneself as the belonging of another. You are Catori. And of all people, you know what that name means. Spirit. If it weren't for the good spirits and even the bad... you would not be here. A spirit is unseen as it is everlasting as one's soul. Within your spirit is the willpower and strength to be chief someday. Spirit is life. The new beginning of a story that writes itself each day." He never thought of it that way because there had always been so much to uphold. He felt that he needed to mirror image his father and if he didn't, then he would be traded off for someone else. Someone better. Grandma pointed to the cloths.

"You want to stay busy and out of sight for a little while? Gather those tunics and other coverings and let's bring them to hang on the branches out there. Let's go," she already started gathering them and continued on as he scampered behind with dripping wet clothes that caused goosebumps to spread all over his body. It was strange because she was headed towards the coast and not the forest where there would be many branches.

Abornazine

7

"Where are we going?" Catori called after his grandmother. She was very stubborn and didn't respond, just continued on. They went past the pond that they had just been at. Specks of grass poked through the melting snow. The sun's blinding rays caused him to look down at the ground instead of ahead. Even then, the light reflected in the patches of snow that were left from the previous snowfall and still partially blinded him from the brightness. Just as they passed the stream, he could tell exactly where she was headed and it was towards the shore by the island. He decided to stop asking questions and just followed her quietly.

"There is one story that you have not heard before. I think it is time," she said, venturing further. When they reached the sand near the shore, her careful steps slowed down until she set some of the clothes over a rock and gestured for him to do the same. They both sat down on a couple of the rocks that formed the meeting circle for their tribe. All was quiet except for the waves washing ashore then retreating in a continuous dance. Grandma looked out at the island and stared, not speaking a word. It looked as though she was waiting for something to appear and he could tell she was deep in thought. Catori did the same. They both sat there for a while and just looked. He didn't want to disrupt her from her peace even though he was anxiously awaiting what she would say next.

"Before your father's time, we used to go to the island very often. The low tide brought a pathway that would tempt just about anybody to follow it down and the only thing we had to be careful of was coming back before the tide came back in, concealing it," she looked out at the island and Catori could almost feel the desperation in her voice as it seemed like she wished she could flash back to those times. But what had changed? If they could go there all of the time back then, why couldn't they go any longer?

"So why doesn't Pa like it? I mean…the spirit that was there before I was born, warned him to turn back and actually helped him before the tide came in." Catori pondered this all the time and was glad he had grandma to speak to about this.

She let out a long sigh and stood up, walking towards the edge of the sand where the water trailed up. Bending down, she took one shell in her hand and washed it off before standing back up to further inspect it.

"Well?" Catori insisted. He followed her over but didn't come as close to the water as she did as her deerskin boots were getting wet.

"In my time, it was a nice place to go but also a dangerous place, too. I would visit my grandmother there because our ancestors protect that land. But the good spirits are not alone. This is something you cannot see with your eyes, but it is a darkness that overcomes oneself if they have no direction in life or purpose." A tear streamed down her cheek as if she knew someone personally who had been lost to that darkness. She continued.

"Your father had a brother. They would go there quite often. His brother was different from him, but it could have been due to envy for not being next in line to be the chief of our tribe." Catori turned to his grandma, questionably. *Why hadn't he heard of this story before?*

"They were rivals their entire lives. Each would try to wake up earlier than the other to go hunting with their father. When he was around your age, he began hunting on his own - almost like he felt the need to prove that he could to others. It was a great help in many ways because this competition supplied our tribe with a lot of food." She stopped and put her hands on her hips, staring out again.

"Why didn't he tell me that he had a brother?" was all Catori could think to ask. She ignored his question and continued.

"When your father was given the right to be chief shortly after your grandfather passed, Abornazine left the mainland for the very last time. You see, he had been able to come and go but I think that was the final point of which he felt he could not return." She paused for a moment, clearly allowing Catori to take it all in. He knew that Abornazine meant keeper of the flame. It was a symbolic name in that flame could represent the light in this world, but you could see it from the other side as well...a darkness and destruction. Grandma broke her gaze from the island and turned to Catori, taking his hands in her own.

"Before you were born, your father would still venture out there to sometimes see his brother and hunt, too. But the more he went, the more he could see that his brother was lost until one day, he was barely able to recognize him and distinguish him from an animal. The evil spirit had taken over Abornazine and he was no longer himself. There was no way to stop this as the spirit needed to live in someone's body. That is when he knew he could never go back there," she finished. They both just looked out at the island in complete silence, still holding hands. If it weren't for the sound of the crashing waves and seagulls soaring above, you would've been able to hear their shallow breaths. She looked into his eyes and he had never seen his grandmother more serious than now. Her eyebrows were pulled in, worry spread across her entire face.

"Some nights, you can hear his screams at the moon. This is why you cannot ever go there; you understand?" She said, looking him right in the eyes.

Dances Under the Moon

8

When they headed back into village, Catori could not shake the thought of Abornazine from his mind. Why hadn't his father ever spoken to him about his own brother? In a way, it was like he was banished...but then grandma said he ran away on his own. Before they got back, she made him promise not to speak about it to anyone at all.

He could smell the venison burning on a wooden stick over the fire. It was custom to skin the deer then tie it so that it could cook over the heat. They carved off a few pieces to store for another feast so that it could last them through the next few weeks. The story his grandmother told him had taken his mind completely off the buck, but now he thought about how its life was lost and its family would not recover from that loss. He turned to his right and grandma had wandered off somewhere which she was keen on doing.

"Hey, wait up," Aponi yelled from behind. She slowly jogged until she was by his side and they continued walking towards the long house. She wore the same long boots, but this time had a light brown tunic on instead of the fur covering. The day was slightly warmer, but they were in the midst of winter - worse storms were yet to come. Aponi's freckled face was covered in delicate, red and black face paint. Its intricate design scrolled in curves up and over her eyebrows. They stretched into spirals around and down onto her temples. On the lengths of the lines and spirals, red leaves and flowers were painted on from each side. This meant that their feast together would be more of a celebration, but he wasn't sure what it would be for.

"I heard what you did today, nice job!" She applauded him.

"What, something I should have been doing all along? Hunting?" He was quick to brush off the compliment. Aponi sped up her pace and stood in front of him, stopping him in his tracks. Even though he towered over her, she stood firm and took his bicep in her grip.

"You didn't just hunt and bring back any game. This buck is going to last us for a while and when the storm comes, our tribe will be well fed. You have eased many worries of the people," she looked down for a brief moment and then brought her attention back up to his eyes. "So accept the compliment, for tonight we will celebrate together."

This was a different side of Aponi that he had not seen in a while. She always pushed him to be better but was not usually as stern as she had just been. They would often joke around with one another and were rarely serious.

"Catori!!! Nice job, man!" A group of guys walked past them and patted him on the back. The last one in their pack turned around and made a kissing face, of course mocking him and Aponi. At that point, Aponi's grip on his bicep loosened and they too trailed in the same direction the pack headed.

Walking into the long house was a completely different ambience than it had been previously. As soon as he entered, all eyes turned to him. Pa stood up from where he sat in the ritual circle and sauntered in his path. His demeanor was vastly different — he even put his arm around his son and walked him towards the middle of the circle while everyone else knelt. Aponi took her spot beside her parents who were already kneeling down. All eyes stared right at him and his father, center of the room.

"My son...this feast is to the thanks of his triumph hunting today. We will be set for a couple weeks and do not have to worry. You are following your path of becoming chief someday," father said as he picked up a bowl full of red dye that closely resembled blood. He drenched his entire hand in the deep red dye and when he brought it out, signaled Catori to take off his fur covering so that the only thing covered was his lower half. Father pressed a handprint of red on one side of his bare chest. Dipping his other hand in the dye, he then pressed a matching handprint onto the other side of Catori's chest. Grandma walked over and brought a different dye that was much darker and started drawing two lines that connected to one another again and again on his shoulder. They resembled the back of the arrow that he had used to kill the buck. She pressed her palm into the liquid again and added to the mural of handprints that he now had but pressed it onto the length of his forearm. She did this a second time just as her dad did and added one to his face, covering half of his lips in a murky blackness. As if this had been previously planned, mother came up and took the darker liquid from grandmother and added two more handprints to his torso below the ones that father added. When Catori and his father were the only two still standing, his father took the remaining red dye and gently painted it over the right half of his face.

"Let us thank our ancestors and the earth for giving us this food. We must not forget to thank this buck for his sacrifice for his spirit will live on through us," he said signaling for Catori to kneel down alongside him. But this time, he knelt with his father in the center of the circle. His mother had a radiance beaming from her and he could tell that she was proud of him without her having to say any words at all. Her eyes were shut. Next to her was his grandmother. Before closing her eyes, she winked at Catori and smiled. He too shut his eyes knowing his prayer was likely much different than his people's.

I am thankful for all that you have given me. I will give back by taking care of the life that I have but also the lives of others. Even more so, I apologize for taking away from the deer family. We rejoice at this time while others mourn for their loss and scavenge for any remnants of grass or food that they can find. Please protect my tribe for I will try my best to protect the earth.

After the prayer, he was astonished to see that everyone already had their eyes open and they were just waiting on him. Pa pulled Catori up to stand alongside him and noticed that he gestured over to some other men in the group.

The next thing he knew it, he could feel a large headdress placed over his head. As the same headdress had been worn by every chief, the top barely fit over his head and if it weren't for the other tribesmen tying it in the back, it would have surely fell to the floor. The women of his tribe crafted it with various feathers, deer hide, furs and plants native to their territory. Coming down from each side were long pieces of fur that resembled that of the buck's that he had hunted. This light brown fur must have been from another hunt and kept for sacred purposes. Although Catori couldn't see himself wearing the headdress, he knew every part of it as his father wore it from time to time when there was a celebration. Feathers that had been mostly white with black tips symbolized the good and the bad. The array of feathers were connected and woven into a piece of deer hide that had elaborate designs in shades of dark red, beige and purple.

"My son will one day take over for me as chief and he has proven that he is almost ready for that responsibility. Today, we celebrate!" And just like that...the ritual began. While some gathered venison and more food to feast on, others danced around him. Grandmother was one of the first to start banging on the drum that was purely made of wood and deerskin. The others joined in. Pa walked off with his mother to watch from the side while he started his people's ritual dance. Catori began by picking his feet up and extended both arms up and to the right then swayed them down and up to the left. This was the dance of the sky. He continued waving his arms in the same motion and circled around the center of the long house. When he came around the circle the third time, he crossed his arms over his chest and took small steps to the left and then the right, turning in a circle and then repeating the same move. As he ran in place slowly, he picked up each of his legs higher and higher, jumping around from front to back in the center of the room. The guys who had previously cheered him on by shouting and howling like wolves in the room, joined in and their shadows mirrored every movement on the wall that was illuminated only be the few flames set out around the room since the sun had already gone down.

Mato had taken out his wooden flute as he commonly did when there was a celebration. He began playing in a long and high-pitched melody. Beside him was Aponi who patted a much smaller drum than his grandmother had. The light from the fire next to her gave the illusion of a warm glow that surrounded her and that he knew was within her as well. As he circled around again in his dance the next time, he found that

Aponi brought her drum to the middle of the long house to join in on the dancing. Her long hair was no longer in braids and instead, hung down tracing over the curves of her body. With each pat of the drum, she moved towards him then back. He reflected her movements as he brought his body towards her then back again. She set her drum down in the center of the room and they used this as a guide to dance around, pulling their knees up and jumping around in a circle. She threw back her head in laughter. They would do this dance as children all the time — he couldn't help but smile either. In this moment, all worries washed away and it was just them in the center of the room with the warmth of the flames shining in.

Lost in Wonder

9

"You and Aponi were killing it out there," grandma budded in as Catori helped himself to some venison. She had the biggest grin on her face causing her face paint to crack in various places.

"Thanks, grandma." He said trying to brush it off so that she didn't fall into the never-ending questioning of whether or not he liked his long-time friend. She walked over with him towards the wooden seats and they sat down. He tried to force himself to eat the venison, but it made him want to vomit having seen the family it was once with...even though he showed his appreciation; it was still difficult. Grandma pressed her cold palm down on his knee.

"It is going to take some time, but you will eventually be okay with this. Look over there," she gestured over towards Pa. He looked overjoyed with a smile that stretched from ear to ear. Pa's soft brown eyes radiated his own happiness out from within. Catori couldn't remember the last time he saw him as happy.

"I know, grandma. I am happy," he knew that fib wouldn't pass by her but still tried anyway.

"You can't fool me! Oh by the way, I think your little girlfriend finally has the feels for you," she joked. Catori's eyes wandered off to Aponi who was also eating some venison. Again, she sat near some of the lit lavender as she spoke with some of the other girls. Just as he was about to pull his eyes off of her, she caught him staring and they locked eyes. He smiled and felt his cheeks grow red in embarrassment but quickly looked back towards grandma who had caught the entire exchange. She chuckled and walked off, leaving him to wallow on his own.

After a while, less and less people were in the long house as they went off to their own homes to sleep. Catori helped to clean up from their feast together, but most pitched in a hand to assist before leaving. The only thing left to do was take the cooked venison that remained and store it somewhere so it could stay cold. It was also important to cover it with other scents so that any bears or other animals wouldn't dig it up. They would pack the food into small clay urns then bury it. This wouldn't attract the bears and would also keep rodents out.

"Thank you for your help today, Catori." His mother called over as she headed out of the long house. He followed her out so they could walk back home together. Pa had already walked back with grandma - the last thing she was was a night owl.

"Yeah it's no problem," he said. "I feel like I haven't seen much of you today, what did you do?" He asked. Everything in him wanted to share with his mother the fact that he knew about father's brother, Abornazine. But he had made a promise to grandma and intended on keeping it.

"Oh you know, just trying to portion everything we gathered from the summer to ration it out for the remainder of winter. That venison really helped us so much, I was afraid we would fall short a few of these nights," it was dark and he couldn't see very well but could tell that she was smiling just from the way that she spoke.

"These past few days, you have really changed a lot, Catori. But I always knew you had it in you." When they reached their home, they both stopped before going in.

He gave her a hug and then they entered. Pa's obnoxious snores filled the room and they grimaced at one another, but mom went on to go to sleep as Catori walked over to his bed and did the same. Or tried to at least...

His father had been keeping one of the biggest secrets one can keep from him and maybe even his mom...he wasn't sure. In fact, no one in the tribe had ever mentioned Abornazine. Was this something they all agreed on? Did Abornazine feel abandoned and lost? Maybe he went out there hoping that someone would come bring him back? But grandma voiced the fact that Abornazine was no longer recognizable as a human... The thought raced in his mind...

Lost Soul

10

Panting. All he could hear was a repetitive panting ringing in his ears. His feet were wet and bare, but there was a figure before him. A woman. Her long, wavy hair hung down below her back. Although it was dark, the moonlight reflected against its raven-colored strands, leaving him with only one guess as to who it was.

"Aponi?" He stuttered through his trembling lips from the cold.

She glanced back at him and paused for a brief moment to smile but continued on without a response.

His eyebrows furrowed in, frustrated and confused... he stopped to try to think of what could be happening. They were just dancing together and then he went home. It was night, so she was going for a walk?

She turned passed a tree and was out of his sight, causing him to pick up his pace again, trailing after her.

"It's not safe out here this late, Aponi. Come back!" He called out in the general direction where he thought she was. He kept going beyond the tree that she had just walked by and still couldn't see her but could hear her steps as she packed down the snow with each stride. Instead of continuing to call out to her, he listened for her steps. She didn't normally play a game like this with him so it was strange, but he needed to make sure she was okay.

After following for several minutes, the trees stood in the background behind them and he could see her much more clearly although her back was still turned towards him. She was headed for the coast right before the path to the island. In fact, she went all the way up to the very last sliver of sand, making it look as though she was about to embark on a journey down that path which he knew she wouldn't dare to do. She was even more cautious than him when it came to curiosity. Aponi turned around and smiled at him.

"Come here," she said, giggling and paused for a moment. The reflection of the moon on the water cast a similar glow on her face as the flame did earlier. This time, Catori felt a different way when he saw her, though. The paint from before still embroidered her face. Her smile brought one to his own face that he couldn't help. He shook his head at the childish game that she was playing, but slowly crept towards her. When he got about two arms' distance away, he knelt down and wet his hand in the rising waters. Catori touched his wet fingers to her forehead, wiping the paint away. His initial touch sent a shiver down her spine with its frigid shock. It took a few times for him to repeat the routine, but eventually the design that was once spread across her skin was no more and all he could see were her delicate features. Although she had a deep-black shade of hair similar to that of the rest of the tribe, she had deep brown eyes, fair-white skin and thin lips pressed firmly together.

"What are we doing here?" He finally asked. She clasped her hand around his wrist that had just been on her forehead and pulled him closer into her.

"I want you to take me here," she whispered and gestured over to the island. The once playful look on his face disappeared as he was left speechless. Why would she want him to take her there? Didn't she know of the warnings and danger?

"I can't do that," he said, looking down. What happened next was something he never would have guessed. She simply turned around and started walking across the path that was now visible and led all the way down to the island. He took a long stride towards her and put his arm around Aponi, leading her in the opposite direction - back to their tribe. She managed to duck under his grasp and then started sprinting towards the island. He had no choice but to sprint after her.

He was sure that he was a much faster runner than her, but for some reason he couldn't catch up. He almost felt like he was going in slow motion. When they were just halfway to the island, a loud screech came from it, causing bats to swarm around the sky above the bare trees that towered over the land.

"Aponi, what has come over you? We cannot go there, you know that!" He called after her. Nothing he said seemed to have any sort of effect on her. She knew what she wanted and she was going to do it no matter what even if Catori couldn't understand why.

They came to the end of the path and Aponi slowed down into a walk so he was able to catch up to her. There were several colossal boulders in various places. He could not see out to the other side since the bushes and trees stood in the way. It was much vaster than he ever imagined.

A similar screech came from within the center of the island and then echoed until there was complete silence. Not even the sound of the waves crashing around them filled the air. Aponi paused and stared right at one of the bushes. She put both her hands out as if she was sacrificing herself and in the next second, a monstrous creature appeared from that bush, its back covered in a thick sheet of snow as if it had been dormant for some time. It pounced, pushing her onto her back and knocking the breath out of her so she couldn't even scream. Its long, gray fingers pushed down on her neck while it sunk its fangs into the flesh on her shoulder. All too soon, it began ripping the skin off her bones. Catori lunged towards the beast and pushed and kicked and tried everything he could to get him off of her. It had numerous antlers poking out from its head, but that was the only part of it that resembled a buck. Otherwise, its body was wolf-like. He grabbed a hold of one of the antlers, pulling it back but it did not make much of a difference. Instead, he fell onto his own back. Catori finally walked over to the edge of the land and grabbed any kind of rock he could find that had a sharp edge. With this, he ran towards the creature again and started smashing the rock into its head. It did not even flinch.

"Stop!" Catori shouted. The beast retreated back a few steps and stared at Catori. He looked down at Aponi's lifeless body that had just been partially destroyed. There was nothing he could do. He tried fighting and barely made a dent— nothing seemed to have an effect on this monster. It moved each of its front paws back like it was getting ready to pounce on him too. Catori's body was frozen with fear. The moonlight started to reflect more and more on the island as the clouds that had been in front of it slowly moved away. He noticed that it was not the moon at all. The glowing outline of a buck emerged from the forest within the island. It reminded him of the buck that he had killed. The buck had the same splash of white under its neck and white around its eyes as well. What was different this time about it was a handprint on the side where his arrow had shot through. The buck walked over to his side and Catori pressed his own hand against the handprint that was marked on its side. It lined up perfectly as it was no bigger or smaller than his was. Being that it did not charge at him and stood on his side against the creature that he had never seen before, he was no longer alone. Its spirit lived on. The buck stared straight through Catori and they were just a step away from one another. Instantly, Catori felt a powerful sensation run through his legs and up his torso to the point that he was now ready to face this creature head on.

The wolf immediately stopped revving up to lunge towards Catori. The buck tipped his head down and started charging towards the beast. The world around Catori grew lighter and lighter until all faded and nothing remained.

Water began to fall onto his face. He wiped it repeatedly and rubbed his eyes. When he finally reopened them, he was in his bed at home with his entire family standing around him. Grandma had a water pale that she had just poured onto his face. He instantly sat up.

"Aponi, Aponi?? Where is she?" He asked, more alert than ever before.

"She is ok, she's home. You had a bad nightmare, that is all," mother said as she rubbed his back. He gulped down hard. He was relieved, but still more scared than ever before.

Unstoppable

11

No one could stop Catori from leaving to go find her. He was not going to believe she was ok until he saw it with his own eyes. He left his family in a deep confusion as he headed out of their home, although no one called after him. Once he got his mind set on something, it was difficult to turn back at that point. In his rush, he had forgotten to put something warmer on. As soon as he made it out into the cold, wintry air, he could feel the goosebumps along his arms and legs. Catori picked up his pace into a sprint over towards

Aponi's home. It was just a few houses away and mirrored all of the other smaller wigwams surrounding the longer one that his people congregated at during ceremonies. He slowed down his sprints when he got to the entrance and moved the deerskin aside to find an emptiness that ran deep in his core. Not even her mother or father were inside the home. He ran out and went towards the coast. Whenever he couldn't find Aponi, that is where he went because odds were that she was cleaning various items with her favorite lavender. He could feel his heart racing in his chest and although it was below freezing outside, his palms were full of sweat. He kept telling himself that she was okay and not to worry as his family assured him before.

His mind flashed to a memory of them when they were just children. In the dead of the winter, they would bring so much life to everything around them. At the time, daylight was coming to an end as the sun's rays beamed through the bare trees. It caused the snow to glisten which felt as though they were in some magical land. Aponi had made a crown out of bark that she would bring with her and place over her head. As soon as the crown was on, she was the snow princess. They would build a fort within the woods and it was his job to protect their fort from the other kids.

"Oh no," she yelled out and threw her hands up to her head. "My crown has been taken!" And just then, one of the boys was running away, laughing as the others cheered him on. Catori naturally took the responsibility to look out for and protect her. Even from boys that were just playing around.

He had created a pile of snowballs for this sole purpose and ran over to it to begin the big fight. He threw snowball after snowball and perfectly targeted the one boy that had stolen Aponi's crown. He brought back his arm and pinned the snowball directly in the middle of the boy's torso. As soon as it struck his body, the crown fell from his hands and the boy collapsed on his side. The other boys began directing their own snowballs towards them. As they did this, Catori felt a presence join him as they sat by his side. Aponi looked over at him and smiled as she laid her hand open, expecting something to be placed in the cup of her palm. Catori took a snowball and placed it in her grasp.

"Quick, hide!" Catori called out to Aponi as they both moved their positions to hide behind a tree that extended up from a colossal trunk. He looked her way for a brief moment and smiled at her as she exchanged the same look back to him. If she was the chief, she would be fair but also understanding. She wouldn't be the type that sat back and instead would join in and help the others no matter how physically demanding the job was. He admired that quality.

After several rounds of snowballs hit the other team,

they shouted that they surrendered. The one boy that had

taken the crown was now lying flat on his back, against

the snow. He extended his arm out with the crown

grasped in his hand.

"Wait here, I'll get it. Be ready in case we are

ambushed again," Catori told Aponi. She nodded her head

in agreement.

He took long strides over to the boy who had been

laying there the entire time, limp. Maybe they went a

little overboard with all the snowballs. He took the crown

out of his hand.

"Why don't you just join us, hmm?" He asked Mato

who still lie there on the ground.

"I don't know, she's your girlfriend!!" Mato said,

mocking his friendship with Aponi as always.

"No she's not," he retorted back reaching his arm out

to help Mato up. He was much more weight than he

thought and he had to use his other arm to pull him up all the way.

"Ok whatever you say," Mato said as he headed the other direction to reconvene with the group of boys. Catori had rolled his eyes and walked back over to Aponi.

She was in the hut that they built out of long sticks. Her heavy fur poncho was almost like a dress on her. The few flakes of snow that drifted down from the sky had latched themselves onto her hair. They shimmered in the light's reflection. He walked over and placed the crown above her head and in that moment, the entire cold world around them grew warm and it was just as it should have been.

Catori finally got up to the coastline to search for Aponi. Although that memory of his was good, it was the last that he had of them together as children. After that, he felt pressured to join into the other boys' activities. It wasn't until they got older that they began speaking again. Even though she was trained in gathering and cooking like the other women did, he would sneak late at night to teach her skills that would normally be taught to the boys of the tribe. One of the skills that she wanted to learn the most was hunting.

Just past the boulder, Catori let out a deep breath as he saw Aponi leaning against it from the other side and creating a design in the snow with a stick.

Marking

12

When Catori finally found her, he was relieved to see it had all been a horrible nightmare. Unable to control himself, he ran over and wrapped his arms around her, pressing her head into his chest. She wiggled out and looked confused, as her eyebrows creased up.

"Have you gone out of your mind?" she stepped away and questioned him. He hadn't told her about the dream that he had. Although Aponi was okay, it still didn't change the fact that Abornazine was no longer recognizable as a man and turned into some creature that was forever lost on the island. It was difficult for him to keep this from his father who had to have known as well.

"I'm just glad to see you," he was still hesitant on sharing his dream with her. She shook her head and rolled her eyes.

"Well, when you're ready to tell me what is really going on, I'm all ears," there was no getting by her. When Catori finally found her, he was relieved to see it had all been a horrible nightmare. It still didn't change the fact that Abornazine was no longer recognizable as a man and turned into some creature that was forever lost on the island. It was difficult for him to keep this from his father who had to have known as well. They sat against the boulder for a while and he stared out at the island while she continued drawing in the snow.

"Promise me you'll never go out there?" He turned towards her. He knew that she wouldn't believe him at first as he was usually the one to try to go to the island. He wanted more than anything to tell Aponi about Abornazine but had to stay true to his promise to grandmother.

She put her stick down to the side and looked directly into his eyes. Their softness calmed him down and the other worries he had seemed to wash away as the waves went to and fro against the shore. These waves took his problems and sent them away… away to the island, which was his main worry. He focused back on her eyes and saw the familiar deep brown that felt warm and inviting. In the next moment, her eyebrows creased together as if she was in question and confused about something.

"What is it, you've always wanted to venture out there. What has changed?" She had the same perplexed look on her face when they were just children and he said he couldn't hang out with her any longer. He still felt sorry for this and there was so much missed time that he could never get back. For what? To be a friend of the other boys? He couldn't decide if he wanted to share his family's secret to her.

"I just had a very bad dream about you going out there and something happening to you. It's against the tribe anyway — it's best we just don't go there," he chose to keep it a secret for her own safety and also keeping the oath that he had made about Abornazine. What good was his word if he couldn't keep it? This was difficult because he was used to sharing everything with Aponi.

"Are you sure that's all?" She could read right through him and definitely knew there was more to the story. Catori nodded and knelt beside her, reaching his arms out and pulling her into him. She brought a warmth to him that he was missing. This embrace had been different than any hugs that they ever shared previously. He rested his head on her shoulder that was mostly covered by the fur she had been wearing. Her fur shawl gently slid down her shoulder to the point that he rested his head against her skin. When he turned his head in, he could smell the sweet scent of lavender that she must have bathed in. There were a few dark freckles spattered about in various places on her shoulder. The other side of his face brushed against a rough patch of skin.

"What happened?" He asked, bringing his head up to see what it was. A wide cut that looked as though it was still healing was marked on the front of her right shoulder and extended down her collar bone. Her skin was bruised around it in deep purple blotches. Catori had to squeeze his eyes shut and reopen them several times to ensure that he was really seeing the sight before him. Within the purple blotches of bruising was a marking similar to that of a human-like mouth print.

"Do you mind?" He asked and she shook her head to let him know that it was okay to inspect the scar. He gently touched the fur covering and moved it aside a little more to reveal the entirety of the wound. She trembled even by the slightest touch.

"When did this happen?" He asked again, persistent. The scar matched up exactly with the dream except she was still living... It was in the same spot that the creature had gone for first when he began tearing her apart. He shuddered and could feel the goosebumps and hair stand up on his arms except this time it was not because of the cold. Telling her about it would only make her more upset and anxious. It wouldn't do any good.

"I don't know, I woke up with it," she seemed just as troubled. If she only knew.

"Does it hurt?" He asked.

"Only if I touch it," Aponi answered. He held out his hand for her to take and knew he had to bring her to grandmother. Everything lined up too perfectly and he was afraid that parts of his dream were in fact true.

Cursed

13

"Where are we going?" Aponi asked as he brought her back through the woods and towards their tribe. He was in a rush because he wasn't sure what to do next. He knew exactly how that dream ended and didn't intend to allow it to happen.

"Come on, I don't want anyone knowing about this. It'll heal," she said. He ignored her and still continued towards his home. The sun was setting so it would be time to eat soon. He could see everyone gathering near the long house in the center where they usually feasted.

She managed to pull her arm out of his grip so he stopped. She crossed her arms, not one to obey when nothing was explained to her. He should have known better, but this was urgent.

"Just trust me," he said calmly as he extended his hand to her. "I'll explain everything when we get there." She kept her arms crossed in front of her and began walking away. No way was he letting her out of his sight again when this had just happened. He jogged in front of her and pressed his feet firmly into the snow, gently reaching out to her and placing his arm on her unscarred shoulder. At this point, they were behind one of the many trees in the forest so no one could see them.

"I haven't been completely honest about everything. Something happened last night and I think you are in danger. The only person that can know for sure is my grandmother. But I promise when we get to her, I'll explain everything," he was desperate. He didn't even know if she would believe him for sure if he did tell her the story.

She stayed there, staring into his eyes. At that point, he crept closer to her and took her face in the sweaty palms of his hands. He looked into her eyes and wished he could lay beside her under a blanket in a much calmer state so that he could take in their beauty. He didn't care to look over his left or right shoulder, but instead the pounding of his heart sent him forward into her so that his lips pressed against hers. At first, their eyes remained open and he noticed that hers widened in shock at the unexpected kiss. He wasn't sure if it was wanted or if she would just slap him and walk away, but something in him finally sent him to make things that he only ever imagined into a reality. In the next moment, she closed her eyes and pressed into him, pulling away gently but pressing her lips into his again and then again. Catori saw stars even though it was daytime and night had not enveloped the skies yet. He was in a whole

new place and for a short time he had forgotten about

the nightmare that had become true. He felt her hands

reach up to his face and place them against his rigid

jawline. It made him lose control all the more and he

moved his hands down her torso to her waist, pulling

her even closer into him. She backed away and blinked a

few times as if to make sure he was still there.

"Come with me, Aponi," Catori said remembering his

priority despite how difficult it was to ignore the

thrilling sensation that ran through the entirety of his

body.

She nodded her head and followed him to his home,

hoping grandmother was there so that they could speak

to her alone.

When they walked past the long house on the way,

the pack of boys called out to the two of them. Mato was

in the back smiling and held the wooden flute in one

hand while the other held a rabbit that he must've hunted earlier on. Another time that Catori missed out on hunting.

"You two on your way to get married finally or what?" They both ignored them and continued on. They made kissing sounds as they walked passed them and Catori and Aponi smiled at one another, reminiscent of a few moments prior.

When they got to his home, he walked in first with Aponi following behind.

"Grandma?" He called in.

"Catori?" She answered and came out from behind the bed.

"What are you doing?" He asked, instantly intrigued.

"Oh, I was just looking for something." She held it in her hands and looked up, taking a step back when she saw Aponi walk out from behind him, waving shyly.

"Hey there, I had a feeling you both would wander in here together," she said. Grandma turned to Catori to finish her sentence. "I'm sure there is something you intend to talk about. Let's go over here to talk. Your parents are preparing the feast for everyone in the long house so we still have some time before they come looking for us." The disheveled blankets that were piled on his bed made it completely obvious that he had been in a rush when he woke up. Grandmother walked over towards it. Aponi took one look at it then turned to him and smirked. Catori put both his arms up and mouthed *What do you want from me?*

"Come on, right over here," Grandma set some incense on the center table and we knelt around it together. The very tip had a fiery glow and sent whisks of lavender smoke up into the air that reminded him of Aponi's soft skin.

"So what is it you have to show me?" She asked them. They glanced at each other and seemed to come to an agreement without a single word. He was going to leave this to Aponi. She did exactly as he thought she would. She stood up before both of them and untied her fur poncho, letting it drop to her feet. Beneath was a light badge tunic made of deerskin, it almost matched the color of Aponi's skin. She gently touched her palm to the cut then winced. Grandma walked over to her and after they locked eyes for a moment, she slowly pulled a bit of the tunic away, revealing the mouth print in its entirety. The same purple hues of discoloration made up the area around the print while Catori noticed that the mouth print had two punctures that ran even deeper and closely resembled fangs. She backed away and knelt back down beside Catori.

"Just as I thought..." she looked down and knelt where they had all previously been. She closed her eyes and looked as though she was praying. Aponi looked over to him in question. He shrugged his shoulders. Grandmother was supposed to have the answers that they were looking for, but instead she was just praying to the spirits. He didn't want to interrupt her, but Aponi seemed to not care at this point.

"What does this mean?? What are you guys not telling me?" Aponi asked, still standing.

Catori looked over to his grandmother. "I know you said that it was a family secret, but we need to tell her," he said. He was not going to tell Aponi without his grandmother's permission. Although this was kind of putting her in a difficult place, there was no other choice. Grandmother nodded and shared the same story to Aponi that she had that night with Catori. She told her all about his father's brother, Abornazine. And how he lost his soul through jealousy and eventually went to the island and was no longer recognizable.

"Wendigo," she said. This was something she had not told Catori before. "This is a creature that has haunted the Paugussetts. A creature that used to be a man but lost its humanity and became animal. It is an evil spirit that consumes one's body... and once you are marked, it is only a matter of time until the change occurs. You will be drawn to the island by the next full moon and will complete the change. The evil spirit must consume someone, so the only way out of this curse is for it to take hold of someone else instead." It took Aponi a moment, but something must have clicked and Catori could see the fear in her eyes. She started backing away.

"A wendigo bit me? This is from him?" She asked, pressing her palm against the bite. "This was the nightmare that you woke up from?" She turned to Catori. He didn't know what to say.

"Why would the Wendigo choose her? Couldn't they have chosen me instead?" Catori asked in desperation.

"The evil spirit comes to you in your dreams. It doesn't matter how it chooses its victim, but it likes to prey on the weak and those that do not have a clear path before them. It preys on those who go against certain norms and attempt at making a path for themselves," grandmother explained. Aponi was anything but weak, however she would do many things such as hunting and fishing while the others harvested the three sisters. Grandmother continued,

"Let me ask you something. Have you ever gone out to the island, even halfway there along the path?" she asked as Aponi shook her head right away. There was a brief pause as if she knew that Aponi had more to say. Looking down at her feet in embarrassment, she explained,

"I have been having bad dreams about the island for the past few weeks. There have been strange things happening like a strong wind coming when it had not previously been windy. I would ask others if they felt it and every person around me had said there was not even the slightest of breezes... But that doesn't even compare to the most haunting detail. When I was at the coastline one night looking for Catori, I glanced at the island and had to do a double-take. Red eyes beamed out from the outside of the island and although the pathway was washed up, I felt the steaming breaths of whatever creature had been staring as if it was right next to me. It frightened me so I looked away and when I looked back, it was gone."

"Aponi, why haven't you told me about any of this?" Catori asked. She shrugged her shoulders which was typical of late but understandable. We all hadn't the slightest idea of what to do. Being that grandmother was praying to the spirits, this seemed like something bigger than anything the tribe could solve on their own.

"What does this mean?" Catori turned to his grandmother.

"She has the curse," she looked down.

Gathering

14

They had to go to the feast before his mother came looking for all of them. Their absence would have definitely been noticed. Right before they left, she answered the question that he was sure both he and Aponi had. *How can they break the curse?*

"This happened once before, long ago. There are two ways to break the curse. The first is to kill the original Wendigo..." Catori couldn't do that. It was his father's brother. He wouldn't be welcomed back into the tribe if he did something like that. Even in secret.

"And the second?" Aponi beat him to it. Grandma took in a long breath.

"You have until the next full moon to find the Wendigo and let him mark someone else, keeping him away from Aponi so that he does not complete the change," He looked over at Aponi. She must have known that he already decided on what he was going to do. Grandma seemed to have known too as she continued.

"If you do not break the curse either way, Aponi will herself become a Wendigo," her words were strained as if this took her to a memory in her past where she had to experience this before.

"I know this is the last thing that you want to do, but we need to go to the feast. We cannot let anyone know. They would want to help and from what I have learned, it is best when not many people are involved," she explained.

"What happened when too many people were involved?" Catori's asked, wondering how it could possibly go wrong, although he had some ideas.

"We are the only tribe in this area for a reason. Because we have grown to respect the island and hold it sacred from afar even though it is tempting to venture out there. Other tribes that had resided here before are now unheard of because the entirety of their people went to the island to find this creature so that it would stop taking its people. No one ever saw them again. We had tried to warn their people, but they didn't listen. That is why we have our rule," grandmother slowly bent down and grasped the fur covering that had fallen to Aponi's feet. She placed it over her head as it had once been and tied it in a knot, letting it drape over her shoulders to conceal the mark. Grandmother stood on her tiptoes and kissed Aponi's forehead.

"You are in good hands, this one is good," she reassured her and winked at Catori. His grandmother always had a way of making any situation seem okay no matter how bad it was. But this time, he wasn't sure if it would be...

He wasn't one to put a mask on and conceal how he felt because the others usually saw right through him. Having Aponi there would make this easier. They walked together to the long house. Catori put his arm around Aponi as they walked and let grandmother lead the way. He could see that Aponi was nervous and the worried look in her eyes caused his stomach to turn. His mind flashed back to the buck's family and how scared they must have been, not knowing how they would survive the remainder of the winter without their strong protector. In this case, Catori had to be Aponi's protector and even though he had no idea what to do, he still needed to at least pretend that he had everything together. That is what we do for our loved ones. We bear the brunt of the pain so that they do not have to suffer.

"It's going to be ok; I'm going to take care of you," he said as he touched his fingertips to a loose strand of hair that fell against her face and tucked it behind her ear.

"Let's go in there and have a good night with everyone." Then, Catori kissed her gently on the cheek trying not to make a sound so that grandmother wouldn't notice since her back was towards them. He could feel the shiver that he sent down her spine from his lips as she shook slightly. The rapid pounding in his chest, similar to that of the drums on the night of the big feast, made him want to run away with Aponi and give into what he craved all the more.

"You two love birds back there have to get yourselves together, ok?" Grandmother hollered back. They smiled at one another and headed in behind her.

Everyone was already in a circle. He took a seat beside his father and mother while Aponi reluctantly left his side and sat next to her own parents. As she walked away, she glanced over her shoulder with a pained look on her face. Everyone around them closed their eyes that is except for Catori and Aponi. Instead, they gazed at one another, longingly. The sudden urgency and threat to their lives made them realize how much they desired one another. Just as she had before, worry met her face in a depressing frown. He winked at her just as his grandmother had done earlier. This always reassured him. She smiled and he closed his eyes to take part in the prayer.

Our land is sacred and we must put back what we once took as our own for the land does not belong to us. We belong to the land. The marking shows a curse that is not easily undone, but please great spirits help me to break this curse once and for all so that no one has to

fear. Help my people and Aponi. Help. Me.

As soon as they were done, his father stood up first
as chief and led the line in gathering some of the food.
Catori followed close behind but could feel a tear stream
down his face from the corner of his eye. The prayer
that he said made his desperation even more real.

"There is something that I have been wanting to
speak with you about, Catori. Gather your food and
meet me by the fire," his father said. He continued
walking through the line and didn't bother to look back
at Catori when speaking to him. Was he already onto
him? Catori wanted to go walk over to be with Aponi to
make sure she was okay but had to obey his father so he
followed him over towards the fire pit. A long, mellow
tune surrounded them as its sound lingered throughout
the longhouse. He looked over by the entrance and saw
Mato playing the handcrafted wooden flute-like

instrument. This time, it was not a very uplifting melody and instead, low notes filled his ears one after another. Mato's father must have past it down to him because he had played it when they were children. He remembered the stories that they would tell by the fire by using the shadows in the light to the melody of that flute.

He sat beside his father, but instead of talking they both watched the show - full of shadows against the wall. The dark body of a man stretched out against the bark and walked. His walk turned into a run and another man followed after him. The man that followed, slowed his steps until he stopped in place. The other continued on, without turning back. An island formed below him as he found himself in isolation. Catori recalled this story, but never knew it was a true story of his father and uncle. A woman stood beside the man who stayed behind and a small baby formed in her arms. The man that was with his family put his arms up as if to shout out to the other. No calls of his could be heard. Instead, the pathway to the island had washed up entirely and the man was no longer a man that stood on two legs. His back hunched as he went down on all fours. He howled at the moon like a wolf and the family on the coast had walked away slowly, full of hurt.

Catori looked all about the room to see where Aponi was and she too had watched the entire display. Her body looked lifeless as she now stared down at her feet. He just wanted to go over to her but needed to talk to his father first.

"Catori, I think the time has come." His father snapped his attention off of Aponi. "It is time for you to be chief. You are as ready as you will ever be."

Nightfall

15

There was just one day left until the next full moon.

He needed to spend every second he had to find the

Wendigo, but at the same time he didn't want to let

Aponi out of his sight. If the legend was true, he would

lose her in one day at the last full moon if he didn't do

something to break the curse. His father planned to

have a celebratory feast the following night to name him

chief, but he had more important priorities than even

that. Because it was too suspicious for him to suggest

for Aponi to stay in their home that night, he arranged

to meet her at the longhouse after cleanup. He planned to set up his trap the following day then come back at night to trap Abornazine. He still had no idea how he would find it in himself to kill his father's brother whom he had never met. Although, as grandmother said - he was no longer human. It was too late for him and he couldn't see sacrificing someone for Aponi's sake. Even if he did just to save her, she would never forgive him. When several people were busy filing out of the longhouses to go to sleep for the night, he saw Aponi talking with her parents. She was using her hands to talk as if modeling something to them. He couldn't tell what she was modeling so when he came up, he was able to put the pieces together from her words.

"Tonight, I will sleep here at the longhouse because I am going to clean up from the feast and prepare something special for tomorrow's feast," she looked over at Catori and smiled, weakly. Her parents looked over at Catori and her mother that was basically an older version of Aponi but with darker eyes and grayer hair, gave him a hug.

"Catori, congratulations on everything. Things are looking up for you! Would you be able to do us a favor?" they asked. Catori couldn't even guess what it would possibly be. He nodded anyways. Knowing them, it must have been of great importance to be asking for help. He glanced at Aponi hoping that she didn't share the news with them about her mark.

"Our Aponi her is going to stay the night here and we are worried of her being alone. You two have known each other your entire lives. Would you mind staying here with her so that she is not alone?" she asked. It was a delight to Catori's ears and he now had the perfect excuse to his parents to stay at the long house as well. He looked over at Aponi and smiled.

"Of course! I'm just going to walk grandmother back home and then I'll come back here, okay?" he said. "I'll be quick!"

Catori picked up his pace and told grandmother about his plan that seemed to work out because of Aponi's parents' request, too. He didn't want her to sleep alone in case the evil spirit came to her in her dreams again. Then, he shared his plan of trapping Abornazine.

"And how do you plan on making this trap?" She asked, intrigued. He could tell that she was skeptical of the plan and didn't seem to think that this way would work.

"It is going to hang from a tree and I will have to use bait to lure him out of the bush again. Then, I will let go of the rope so that the trap falls down over him. I will use tree bark and vines for the trap. The sides will be made of sharp spearheads so that he can't escape."

While he explained the trap to her, he felt himself also trying to talk himself into the whole idea. He didn't know what to expect other than the nightmare that he had.

"Then what?" She asked the inevitable question. That part he had not thought about yet. He put his arms up, admitting to the unknown.

"I want to try to save Abornazine if I can. Maybe there is some way to break the curse other than sacrificing someone else or killing him. I can try to show him the light," he said. Their tribe was about peace and handling things by calling for a truce with unity. Other tribes meant to fight if met with an attack, but that was not the Paugussetts. As if grandma had already thought about this, she confirmed what he had been thinking all along.

"You remind him of what it is to be human. You remind him of the good. Do not stop and if he breaks loose, you know what to do," she said firmly. She was giving him permission to kill her other child, but at that point he would be too lost if he couldn't help him.

"Be careful tonight, ok?" She turned to him before they walked into their home. He nodded and gave her a long hug. They both walked in and his parents were already asleep. Grandma and Catori had stayed a while later as she had to collect the various incenses that she liked to place about the room while he had been talking with Aponi and her parents. She wandered off towards her bed while he did the same, having no intention of going to sleep. He had to at least lay in his bed for a few minutes so that he didn't have to explain his plan to his parents, too, in case they woke up. Fur blankets that had once felt comfortable and warm, were suddenly irritating and scratchy. He just wanted to get out already, but still didn't hear his father's snoring so they weren't sound asleep just yet. He extended his arms back and stretched his legs, hearing a crack in his back and turned to the side. He rubbed his fingers against the fur on his bed and thought about the buck that stood by his side in his dream. Why had it been on his side if he was the one who killed it? It had protected him in that moment. Then, he remembered what his father said at one of the feasts. The spirits live on through us as we continue to care for the grounds that we live on.

Just then, an obnoxious snore came from his parent's bed. He waited for a few more and lifted himself up, treading lightly against the grounds — he stopped at the door, glancing back at his father as he now snored endlessly. Below their bed was a long spear only used in case of emergency. He could take it, but if he did it would definitely be noticed by his father unless he returned it before he woke. He was only going to meet Aponi, though. Tomorrow was the day that he would go to the island to set up the trap... He decided to get it anyway, the benefits outweighing the risks.

He carefully lifted the heavy part of the spear up first and froze right next to him as his snoring came to a cease. He opened his mouth slowly and let out a yawn then rolled over to his side, facing away from Catori who couldn't have been more relieved. He continued with the long spear out of their home and headed for the longhouse, not looking back.

Her

16

All was dark except for a small flame in the center fire pit that lingered from its earlier embers. He saw the outline of a body across the way and started towards it, still keeping quiet as he was unsure if anyone else was still here. There was slight movement in the person who sat with their legs crossed and facing the wall of the longhouse.

"Aponi?" Catori asked, continuing to creep forward. The person stood up, their shadow outlined against the fiery glow that the flame created. He could tell from her flowing hair who she was, but there was one thing that stood out and only she could be wearing it. The crown that she had made for herself as a kid. The vines and pieces of wood that she had used to make it were all still intact. She wore the fur covering but as she turned back towards him, it gently fell off her shoulder, exposing the scar. This time, the mouth print was even more defined than before and he could more visibly see the two puncture marks on the top with a gap in between. He winced at the sight of them and couldn't begin to imagine the pain that she must have felt. There were just a few times where he had gone hunting with his father and was attacked by some of the animals. Luckily, his father was able to shoot an arrow through the animal's torso to stop it. One time it had been a coyote when Catori ventured too close to its newborns. This is why the tribesmen preferred to hunt in groups as it was safer.

"Yeah, I'm here," she answered with a faint smile. He thought it best not to bring up the addition of fangs to her scar.

"How are you feeling?" He stopped there and she walked towards him. Her steps were taken in a soft, patient pace as she made her way over. Without a word, she wrapped her arms around his neck and pulled him close to her. Catori looked past her and could see their shadows as they became one. At this point, he was her only hope. She was trusting him with her life. They stood there together, not much different from the two children they had once been years ago - he protected her then and would continue to. If that was his sole purpose for being, he was fine with it.

She did not respond. Instead, her hold on him grew even tighter. He couldn't return the favor; afraid he would break her like a toothpick. He could still smell the lavender and swore they should call that scent Aponi instead. It brought his thoughts to her above anything else. Her head turned slightly into his neck and he could feel her cold, chapped lips press up against his skin. It sent shivers down his spine and he felt a rushing come from his core down his arms and into his palms. This was something he never felt before other than when he had kissed her. But now, it was different. They were completely alone and didn't have to worry about the others.

"What are you doing?" He whispered. His few words were silenced by her fingertips as they pressed against his lips. She continued kissing his neck and as good as it felt, he could tell something was off about her. Catori ignored his gut and gave into her kisses, his body seemed to go numb although they still stood there together. With each kiss, he was pushed back more and more until he could feel the bark of the wall rubbing up against his back. Her hold on him was loosened as her fingertips traced down his shoulders and rubbed the fur poncho that he had on from earlier. Her fingers found their way to the tie that held it on and in a few moments, she had undone the tie and the covering fell to the ground, revealing his bare torso. Her hands felt like ice as they wandered back up his torso and moved her lips down from his lips to his chest where her hands had just been. His mind went right to the thought of this not being Aponi, but then he remembered that they didn't have much time left and that he should try to enjoy what was happening.

With his own reassurance, he pressed his lips into her and pushed himself away from the wall, moving Aponi back against it instead. This seemed to drive her even more crazy than before as she repeatedly kissed his neck, nibbling here and there. She continued touching his torso, tracing her fingers against his chest and bringing them up to his neck then back down again until he didn't feel her hands at all. His eyes had been closed the entire time, but he opened them to find her pulling apart the knot that held her fur covering on and let it drop to the floor, revealing the beige tunic. As he saw her ready to take that off, he took her hands in his own and locked eyes with her. He didn't want her to do something that she may regret. And she did not owe him anything at all.

Aponi came forward and moved her lips next to his ear,

"I want you."

With that, he no longer held back. Catori pulled her shirt up and over her head, kissing her on the neck repeatedly as he moved down her shoulders then breasts. Her head fell back in pleasure as he kissed every inch of her body from head to toe. He grabbed both of the fur coverings and laid them down on the ground for her. She took the hint and rested her back

142

against the soft furs as Catori slowly pressed his body into her, concealing each of her moans with his lips. He guided his hips into her as she did the same and it reminded him of the dance that they had done except this time, their dance was as one. He could tell that she felt the same desire as him by the way that she tilted her head back as they continued. The raven-colored strands of her hair contrasted with her bare skin. He began to kiss each freckle on her body and the passion that he felt had come out from many years of being built up. As Catori brought his lips down her neck and to her chest, her head had tilted back again and he knew to keep going. Every response that she had, made touching her even more irresistible.

He felt as though he was in some other world. He laid beside her and they both just let out strained breaths. Lavender filled the air around him as he realized that she must have started burning some incense before he came over. The scent lulled him into such a calm state that he could barely feel any longer.

It took all of his strength to open his eyes and when he did, she was laying on top of him and started kissing his neck again as she had earlier. The scar that she had was now black, more like a tattoo of some sort on her instead of a scar. In the next instant, he felt as though small wooden stakes pierced through his neck and everything went black.

Dormancy

17

Light. A nearly blinding glow washed away any darkness that just was. He ran his fingers through the tall grass that surrounded him. Each blade of grass had remnants of the morning dew. It took almost no effort to sit himself up as he realized he was in a field. He no longer laid beside Aponi. The snow that had encompassed everything previously was nonexistent. Birds that had gone south filled the trees with their melodic songs. *How hard did he hit his head?*

"Oh, you're finally up!" Called out a voice that he didn't have to think twice about in order to recognize. He looked over to his right and Aponi stood there just as radiant as ever. Her sleek hair outlined her beauty. She was no longer dressed in bulky clothes and a fur poncho, but instead wore a light brown dress made of deerskin. It was embroidered with red, white and black dyes likely used from fruits that the women of the tribe had gathered. Dark fringe hung from the bottom of her dress and she still wore her long boots made from deerskin. They went up just below her knees.

"Where are we?" He asked, rubbing his head. Just a few moments ago, she was in some kind of trance and kissing him uncontrollably. They made love... or was that also just a dream that he had? Now, they were in the middle of what appeared to be summer and no one else was in sight. It was as though they had skipped through time somehow.

"We're on the island!" She said, marveling at her own words. He shot right up and walked over towards her, hearing the waves crash in the distance and seagulls soaring above. Everything he had tried to avoid was now unraveling. Now that Aponi was on the island, the Wendigo could reach her much more easily. He didn't even have his spear. It made no sense though, because he didn't remember walking all this way let alone it being daytime already. The beauty of the island made him want to stay, but where was everyone else? And where did winter go?

"How did we get here, though? I don't remember walking over," he questioned her. Again, she did not seem like herself.

"I brought you, but you were a little bit tired so I helped you get here." She smiled over at him, innocently. He knew that she wasn't strong enough to carry him all the way over to the island. She seemed to sense that he still was not convinced. "It's ok to be here, don't worry. Our ancestors just didn't want us to get lost, but now we are found," she spewed out perplexing riddles that just left him with more questions.

"Where is everyone?" He asked, continuing to rub his head as if he could knock some sense into himself.

"Oh, they'll come. We just have to talk them into it!" She replied. He walked past her and continued pacing around until he found two wigwams just past a few of the trees. They seemed to blend into everything else around so they hadn't caught his eye at first.

"If you stay here, we can have this every day." Aponi continued. "It is always beautiful here and we never have to worry." As nice as it was, he still worried about his family back on the mainland. He couldn't leave them, especially without an explanation as to where he was. There was also the Wendigo that they both had to worry about.

"What's the catch?" He asked her. She seemed as though she was walking on clouds and extended her arms up and around his neck, pulling him close as she had done the night before.

"Well, once the moon comes full circle, you cannot leave. So, we'll just stay here!"

"Are you out of your mind, Aponi??" He said, pulling away from her. He felt an overpowering urge to scratch his neck all of a sudden and as soon as he brought his hand up, he felt two puncture wounds that he faintly remembered from the night before.

"Oh, sorry about that. But that's the only way to keep you here, it's a marking."

"Why would you do that?!" He asked, confused. She just repeated herself again and wrapped her arms around him, it was almost like she was trying to bait him into this trap that he wanted no part of. Although, it could be worse than being with Aponi...a life with her did sound nice. But this wasn't the right way. As difficult as it was to pull himself away from her, he fought the urge and walked past the trees, veering towards the wigwams. He peered back over his shoulder and saw that Aponi was looking down at a pond nearby. He wanted to find who was living in the wigwams so he continued on.

The warmth of the summer air made him feel less lost in whatever this was. Just outside the closest wigwam was a man that resembled his father but was about a head taller and he had hair almost as long as Aponi's. He wore deerskin around his waist and it hung down to his knees. The same red, black and white colors lined his arms and chest that lay open and exposed. He was intimidating from afar and Catori could only imagine how much more so he would be up close. But the man that stood before him was familiar... he could see him through his own father. It was his grandfather.

"Hello?" He stopped walking towards him, unsure of how to proceed. The man turned his way and waived.

"Is it you? Annowan?" He said, putting down the rabbit that he had been cutting. Annowan was Catori's father. He had never met his grandfather in person which was probably why he didn't recall him or his name.

"That is my father," Catori admitted.

The Truth

18

They say the truth will set you free. But what happens after that? What happens when all the truths are set out in the open and you are all there - wouldn't it feel more stuck? You are all there with nothing to do except to face these truths no matter how painful they are. But once you do, overcoming it is like you have climbed the tallest mountain you could ever climb and have finally made it to the top. You are looking out at your life and now have clear vision.

Catori was living in a dream-like state. No explanation for how or when it would be over, but he was just there. There to take everything in. His grandfather was everything that his father ever spoke of. He was a strong, but sentimental soul. A family man. He put his family and tribe first above all else. Together, they sat for a while sharing stories about Annowan until finally, the lingering question came up.

"So how did you find yourself here?" He asked Catori.

"That is a good question." He told him about Aponi and then the conversation was driven to Abornazine...Annowan's brother.

"He was always a bit of a lost soul, Abornazine..." he trailed off and Catori thought he could see a faint tear leave the corner of his eye. They were a light shade of brown that were similar to his father's.

"Abornazine… keeper of the flame. He was meant to do great things even though he was second born. I had hoped for your father and him to be teammates and both carry our tribe through the harsh winters." He said, looking down at the ground.

"Well, what happened to him?" Catori pressed on after waiting a moment.

"He is dead…no longer here with us. Something else took his place," his breaths between every few words were strained as if he was fighting to say more. Catori wanted to hear more of his grandfather's side of the story, though. He longed to put together the pieces so he could have a full picture of what really happened. Before he could ask more questions, it was as though his grandfather had read his mind.

"Here it is peaceful, but we are still trapped. We keep watch over the island… we cannot leave, though. Once a soul dies here, they are trapped. Trapped by the creature that lurks around the outside. The creature is what once was a human. No longer recognizable. Every ounce of what once made it human, stripped away and barely a soul left to remember. This is what our culture knows as the Wendigo. When the soul is lost here, it must stay as it takes on a different form. It is what keeps us trapped on this island." Pieces were finally coming together. But how weren't they harmed by the Wendigo? How is there a village that is safe from him, yet still on this island?

"The Wendigo cannot come here?" He asked grandfather. He then stood up and grabbed a long stick, tracing the sand around them. He made a circle and then a smaller circle within it.

"The clearing in the center of the island will bring you here... and this is the one sacred place for our people that the Wendigo cannot set foot on. We can sometimes leave the clearing, but rarely do as it is outside of our safe space. In the clearing, it is a constant summer and may seem like paradise except for the fact that we are all trapped," he looked down.

"So you are saying that you are a spirit who is trapped here? What happens when you are no longer trapped on this island? Can you go be with grandmother?" Catori asked another question and mentally noted that this would be the last question he'd ask.

"I will be able to rest in peace. My spirit is here, but once set free – I will be able to join the other spirits in our world. I will be able to watch over the tribe. Right now, I cannot rest although I am no longer alive – it is my spirit that is imprisoned. I am just a path away from your grandmother whom I love and would do anything to be with. The torture of not being able to venture back to her is the worst type of suffering that anyone can go through aside from watching their loved one die," He walked over to Catori and gave him a hug, wrapping his muscular arms around him. It made him feel like a toothpick that could be easily snapped in half just as Aponi must've felt when he hugged her.

"When you leave the clearing, be careful and do not trust anything that you see. I will try to have my people help you," he pulled away and patted Catori on the shoulder.

For some reason, Aponi was nowhere to be found while he was there with his grandfather. He looked all over and just couldn't find her.

"Any idea where Aponi ventured off to?" He asked.

"Who?" Grandfather replied. *Weird...*

"The girl that the Wendigo bit, I'll be back soon, I've gotta go look for her," he gave his grandfather another hug then wandered off, heading back where he had first woken up.

"Aponi?" He shouted as he walked through the clearing. He hadn't gotten to the center yet but heard humming from the distance. It was coming from just past a set of bushes and wildflowers growing near a tree. He walked by it to find Aponi, the light beaming down on her. She looked almost heavenly with the way the light cast its rays down on and around her. She continued humming but was just dabbling her fingertips across the water's surface on a pond that stretched out before her.

"There you are," he said, sitting beside her. He didn't bother looking at the pond at all, but instead his full attention was on her.

"Why didn't you come with me? Grandfather was there."

She shrugged her shoulders, "I don't think I can until the change is complete. For some reason, I can only step a few steps outside of the center of the clearing but can go no further. See, this is why I want to be here. All of our ancestors await us. Join me," she grabbed both of his hands in her own and looked him right in the eyes.

"What about everyone else?" He asked.

"What about them?" She said then pulled his body into her own in a warm embrace. He couldn't help but notice that there was still something off about Aponi. And why couldn't she come with him?

"We've got to go back, it's what is right. And we need to figure out a way to stop the curse," he reminded her. No matter how hard she tried to distract him from the plan, he needed to stick to it. She pulled back.

"It's ok, we don't need to stop it," she flashed a smile at him and brought him close again.

"I just want you here with me, ok?"

He was not agreeing to her terms but wrapped his arms around her and stared out at the island's natural beauty. Morning dew from the grass had dripped down and fed its soil. It no longer had a shimmering look, but the sun's rays reflected off the pond next to them. It gave a mystical impression of their surroundings. On the other side of the bushes that stood next to them was a glimpse of something much darker that suddenly caught his eye. A creature's reflection shown in the water. He could see his own reflection right next to that creature as it towered over him with its back arched. Catori squeezed his eyes a few times and reopened them, trying to wake himself up. The creature's head turned slightly and opened its mouth. He could see its wolf-like snout in the reflection of the water and its fangs protruding out of its mouth. Catori pulled away from Aponi and jumped back a few feet.

"Who are you?" He asked.

She smiled and started walking towards him at which point he turned and began running the opposite way - back towards the center of the clearing again. The light around him had fallen abruptly to a grim, pitch black that blanketed the world around. He found himself tossing and turning in the middle of the clearing, but this time it was back to a cold winter's night with snowy white over everything around him. Aponi was again, nowhere to be found.

First Warning

19

Catori felt exposed. He had prepared to bring spears
and several other things to the island so that he could
trap Abornazine. But instead, he laid flat on his back,
staring straight up at the sky as the bare trees towered
over him. He and those trees weren't much different.
They were both stripped of their protection and just
remained. But another thing that they had in common
was that neither of them were alone. Even on this
island, he could still feel the spirits swarm around him.
He couldn't necessarily see them, but they were still

there whether they be the trees themselves or even the island. A few drops of snow trickled down onto his face, melting as soon as they touched his skin. After that, more and more came down. He decided it was time to get up no matter how confused or unprepared he was. He stood in the clearing just as he had before. It was strange because it seemed that this was some sort of doorway into the past to be with his ancestors. He didn't quite grasp it. As much as he wanted to try to go back, he needed to move on and find Abornazine to end this once and for all.

When he stood up, he felt dizzy as it had just been summer and now it was bitter cold in the dead of winter. It was a nice place where he had just been. But it could also have been a trick. As he crept towards the outside of the island, all appeared calm. He couldn't even hear the waves crashing against the shore. Snow came down in a steady parade which made him untie his fur poncho that had been wrapped around him and pulled it tighter around himself. A sound came from up above. It was a calling and it repeated itself again and again. He looked up to see an owl as the moon cast its glow upon it. Catori remembered this owl from when he was young and his father first told him the story about the island. Back then, it had been like his eyes were playing tricks on him. But now, it was just too similar to the owl he had seen before... it had to be the same one. A magical glow surrounded the entire shape of its body and it sat perched upon a branch just above where he stood. He had to keep blinking his eyes so he could see the owl clearly as the snow trickled into his sight.

Before he could get a better look at the owl, it sprung its wings out and swooped down right in front of him. The long, extended wings flapped repeatedly as it stayed in the air. The snow continuously came down on him and the owl alike. Each white drop blended in easily with its white feathers while they landed on Catori's dark hair and stayed there for a few moments until dissolving from his warmth. It seemed to look right into his eyes. Something about this owl struck him as familiar and it wasn't because he had seen the owl when he was young. He felt as though he had seen it just a few moments ago. Unlike any owl he had ever seen before, this one had one distinct feature besides its glowing body. When he stared into its eyes, he couldn't help but notice it had similar light brown eyes to that of his grandfather's. There was a softness in them that reminded him of his father. They were much different than the deep chestnut brown that Catori saw when looking into Aponi's eyes. Could it be that this was his spirit watching over him? As Catori was deep in thought trying to piece everything together, the owl drew even closer towards him, pushing him towards the path to go back to the mainland. As it swooped its wings, it pushed the following snow towards him again and again. It felt as though the owl had been warning him to leave the island, but that was something that Catori just could not do.

Its sleek wings now dusted in snow rose above him and over the towering trees towards the entrance of the island. Catori could tell because that is where he had first come from in his dream when he followed Aponi here. He felt like it hadn't been a dream, but still was unsure. He knew the owl was telling him to go home. He practically led him to the entrance of the island so that he could leave. Instead, he walked in the opposite direction of the owl, focused on completing his purpose there in the first place. He continued on through the darkness, the moon's reflection in the waters being the only light that guided him.

Blended In

20

It was the calm before the storm. The waters
retreated back slightly only to tread up the shores again,
not making much sound on this cold, eerie night. For
Catori, it felt like the longest night that he ever had
because of his finding in the clearing. But now being
back in the correct place, he couldn't seem to find
Abornazine anywhere. Catori wandered through the
island and found himself at the edge where the waters
met the rocky outline. From there, he turned around
and looked at the vast land that stretched out before

him. It looked like it went on forever...but from the mainland, it appeared much smaller. He walked towards the edge where the sand met the water and grabbed the biggest rock that he could find so that he had some form of tool to use against him if needed.

As he looked out, the owl was nowhere to be found. He must've given up on him. Catori didn't blame him, after all he completely ignored his warning. There was one thing he knew for sure and it was that he was not leaving without dealing with Abornazine. The breeze whispered in his ears as they guided tree branches to sway back and forth, causing an unsettling sound that one of the branches was going to snap at any moment.

He thought he heard a faint voice of a woman calling for him, but the undistinguishable words were incoherent as they came out as mumbles. He brushed it off and continued walking around the outside of the island, looking for any sign of the Wendigo. As he kept walking, he heard the sound again and it seemed that he was getting closer to whatever was trying to speak.

"Hello?" He whispered, trying not to be too loud afraid that it would gain the attention of the Wendigo. He wanted to be the one to startle the Wendigo so that he would at least have the advantage of ambushing it. The mumbling continued and he followed it. Continuous groans led him closer to the entrance of the island, which was where the owl was headed. The snow's continuous flakes were slowing down as each flake was a bit bigger than the previous one. Catori could tell the snow was going to come to a stop soon. As he walked more and more towards the mumbles, he had to stop because they too ceased.

"Is someone there," he whispered again. His attention was immediately brought above him to the same owl from before, but it was now perched on a tree, staring down at him. The glow around the owl's body made the area where he stood much more visible. Yet, he still couldn't see the woman who called out to him.

"Where is she?" He called out to the owl. It turned its head to the left, which was again towards the entrance and mainland. Catori continued on, snow covering any tracks that he had made previously. As he looked forward, he felt his legs fall out from under him and dropped face first into the snow. He had tripped over a lump in the snow and couldn't tell because everything had been pure white. The woman that he had been looking for turned out to be under that lump of snow. She let out a groan as Catori laid with his legs on top of her still. He pushed his hands down against the ground to lift himself up again and turned around.

"Are you ok?" He asked, still trying to keep quiet although they had made quite a ruckus.

"Mmm," she let out a moan again still unable to speak for some reason. He turned the woman to her side and found Aponi. She looked like herself, except her face had several scars across it.

"What happened to you?" He asked right away, forgetting to whisper.

"Shhh," she shushed him as she squeezed her eyes shut. She looked like she was in pain. She wasn't even getting up from the ground. When she opened her eyes again, they looked past Catori in horror. Just then, drips of saliva came down onto Catori's shoulder. He turned his head to his right to find that he was face to face with the Wendigo...

Run or Flee

21

Several moons ago, he was walking to go fish. He remembered it being a cool autumn night as the gentle breeze carried the leaves of many colors to and fro. This was a time of year when the earth around him went through its cycle of change. The trees let off their leaves as they were once full of life and green. It was a cleanse for all of nature for after winter came, the trees' leaves would be replenished, birds would come back to build nests and more life would be created. The cycle would continue endlessly. Autumn was the most beautiful time to Catori. Even though winter was before them, it taught him how necessary it was to let go of some things so that you too could cleanse yourself and start anew.

He walked to the same stream as usual. It was peaceful to go alone and not have to worry much. But sometimes, he would invite Aponi along. This was not one of those times. He had just caught a fish and knelt down to take it off his pole so that he could carry it back home. Further inland, there was a harsh growl that echoed through the forest, causing the waters to tremble before him. He quickly turned to see what it had come from. Just a few trees out, stood a dark brown grizzly bear on its hind legs. Behind the bear were smaller cubs running the other way. This was a mother bear protecting its cubs from a threat to its babies - him. Even though he hadn't done anything to its cubs, it still looked at him as a threat. He was bigger than most prey that it sought after and it may have seen another human taking a bear's life. So then it looked at all humans as a threat...especially to its young. He had two options at this point: run and try to climb a tree or stand where he was and make as much sound as he could to scare it off. He chose the latter.

This time when the Wendigo stood next to him, Catori did not have the comfort of the creature being as far as the nearest tree as the bear had been back then. He remembered the two choices that he had with that bear and was quick to choose the same option again and fight... pretend that he was the bigger creature and try to scare it away.

And so there he was... again in a similar situation, but with a much different creature this time. Catori stood up and pushed out his chest to appear as big as he possibly could to this beast. Its eyes were set on him and although Catori was one of the tallest men in the tribe, he still was short by the length of several heads compared to the Wendigo who could measure close to the middle of a tree.

"Don't," Aponi let out a weak yelp before the Wendigo grasped its long, fingers around her side and pushed her out of its way. Although it had a wolf-like snout and snarling fangs protruding out of the sides of its mouth, it also had sharp, pointing antlers poking out from behind its deer-like ears. The antlers looked like they had been pure-white at one time, but a mix of dirt and blood covered them. Being so near to the Wendigo, the smell of rotten flesh filled the air, nearly making Catori gag from the foul odor.

"I am not afraid of you," Catori shouted at it. "We are not afraid." He corrected what he said because in fact, he was not alone. He could see the glimmer of light in the tree that was the owl and he knew there were more where he came from.

"Abornazine, do not let the wendigo win! Come back to us," Catori desperately shouted, not knowing what else to say. The creature just stared at him, licking its teeth as droplets of blood streamed out, staining the pure white snow. Catori looked back at Aponi and could see that there were even more bite marks than there were before. All along her shoulders and neck, dark red had been painted over and concealed her skin. This time, the deep shade of red was her blood as he saw it streaming down the length of her body. When he turned back, the creature stood up on its hind legs as the bear had. The full moon made its face even more visible and Catori could see that its eyes were completely bloodshot. There really was no resemblance to any human at all. But he had to at least try.

Before he could do anything, it took one slow step towards him. It seemed to think that Catori had no chance because otherwise it would chase him. He wasn't going to give into the chase though. It continued

on taking another step… then another. Again, Catori felt

exposed. He felt naked although he was fully covered

from neck to toe. The monster was looking him up and

down as if he was deciding which part of him to eat first.

He had to somehow make this beast remember who it

truly was before it became the creature that now

towered over him.

Humanity

22

When you fall and have no one else to turn to and feel an empty, lonely pit in your chest... you reach to the spirits around you and earth to help guide your way... you think of a good time of the past to help cheer you up. You think of the beauty in life. The unforgettable grace of nature. The cycle that never ends. We never end. Each child is born into a home and as they grow old, they too bring another into this world. Whether or not they bear a child, they still make a mark in this world and everything that makes up where we live.

When they die, their spirit lives on in that being. That never ending cycle is humanity. The memories that we make with others, experiences that we share with one another... they are each special and one of a kind.

That is what makes us human.

The very fact that we fall. That we struggle. We push again and again. Keep trying. We will eventually get better and rise above who we once were. Because failing is what teaches us the most. If it weren't for those mistakes of the past, we would have nothing to compare our good fortune to.

If Catori was going to attempt to remind this creature of who he was before being cursed into the beast... he needed to talk about the person he was once before. Although Catori hadn't ever met Abornazine, he could tell from grandmother's stories as well as just being with his father who he truly was. The way in which he was raised and his culture represented a great part of his being. He thought of the most important thing that he was taught from the moment he had learned how to speak.

"You are Abornazine. You are the son of my grandfather who had put his tribe over everything else in existence. Above that, he put his children. He held you high and wants to see you take care of the land and his people as he raised you to," the beast stopped roaming towards him. Catori continued.

"Your brother is Annowan," at the slightest mention, the beast started towards him again, snarling more than he had before. Catori understood that this was what the evil spirit had feasted on the most: Abornazine's jealousy towards his brother and how we would never become chief. When he got to just a leap away from Catori, he bent down, going on all fours and then all at once lunged past him and onto Aponi instead. She lay there lifeless, not giving out any yelp or plea for help. It sank its teeth into her and looked as though he was finishing what he had started with her.

The moon had almost come up to the highest point in the sky which meant that the change would soon be complete. Aponi would too turn into a Wendigo and he would lose her forever. As the shimmering owl still sat perched on the nearby branch, just watching in horror... another creature that he was all too familiar with crept out of the woods. Through the darkness, Catori could see the gleaming antlers of a buck. This was the same one that had been in his nightmare.

In that moment, he realized this was the buck's spirit that he had hunted. It was there to protect him like it had before... as it raced towards the Wendigo and rammed its horns into it, it only caused the slightest discomfort. The buck retreated back a few steps to gain momentum and then ran up towards the Wendigo again, ramming him.

This gave Catori an open window of time. The buck glanced at him and seemed to wink its eye then turned back to the Wendigo, leading it away from Aponi. Catori rushed over, careful not to be seen, and picked up Aponi in his arms. Her poncho that had once been a light brown was now soaked in blood and a deep red color. She was as light as a feather, Catori almost sent her flying up in the air when he scooped her up. Her arms fell to her sides as she struggled to open her eyes and look up at him.

"Save. Yourself," she weakly groaned. They both knew that he wasn't going to do that. Instead, he ran over towards the front of the island with her in his arms. When he got there, he could see several of the men in his tribe running down the path and onto the island as well. He could tell it was them by their heavy fur covers and at the head of the line was his father with a torch in his hand to light their way.

"Son, you were not supposed to come here," he said. Catori's father had usually been calm and collected. This time, every emotion burst out all at once. His father looked disappointed, angry, upset, but also frightened... frightened for his son and Aponi. As the men felt great pride to protect the others in their tribe, he had never seen his father look as frightened as he was. There was always a mask that he wore, showing his strength to the others and never an ounce of vulnerability.

"I needed to save her. Take her," his father gave the light to another man and took Aponi in his arms. Catori kissed Aponi for what felt like it would be the last time and began to walk away.

"You can't go back there, Catori! He will take you." His father warned. As much as he didn't want to go back to the Wendigo, he knew that he had to in order to stop Aponi from turning. He had the marking, so he too would turn if the Wendigo got to him before the full moon went to the highest point in the sky.

"I'm going to try to put an end to this once and for all. Watch for the buck and owl. They will guide you to the light." The frightened look on his father's face was gone and instead, he looked sad but also proud of who his son had become.

Into the Light

23

As soon as Catori turned towards the island and began walking the other way, he could see the Wendigo's monstrous shoulders as he approached him. The buck was able to hold it off for a short time but couldn't seem to completely kill it and Catori knew why. The evil spirit that took hold of Abornazine and turned him into this creature needed a body to survive in. This spirit could not just simply go away. This is why it had targeted Aponi. She would be next.

It seemed to be aware of the moon's position in the sky and that its time was running out. Catori walked straight towards it, blocking its path to his tribe and Aponi. It stood up on its hind legs and began running upright at Catori instead. In the next moment, he could feel a heavy weight on his chest. Catori felt his back hit the ground. It knocked the wind out of him and he just lay there breathless. He was unable to get up because the Wendigo had pounced on top of him and stayed there, snarling directly in his face. Its bloodshot eyes felt like knives piercing through his own and into his soul. The entirety of its face was covered in various scars over its gray skin. Tangled, black fur poked out from behind its eyes and came out from the sides of its face. The snow fell less and less, but the creature was still covered in many white flakes, conveying its lack of warmth.

That is when he felt the sharp horns of the Wendigo ram deep into his chest. An indescribable pain sent blood rushing to his head. Catori just lay there, lifeless...as Aponi had once been. There was no recovering from these wounds. It then lifted its head and as much as Catori wanted to squeeze his eyes shut as not to see the Wendigo's gruesome face, the darkness was much worse. As he kept his eyes open, it reminded him that he was still alive even though he felt that would be taken away from him too in a very short amount of time. His own blood dripped down onto him from the Wendigo's horns that had just stabbed him through his chest, where his father's red palmprint had marked him. How he wished to feel the warmth of his father's hand again or anyone's hand. The Wendigo licked its teeth as Catori winced at the horrific stench that it breathed out. The Wendigo opened its mouth and sunk its teeth into the mark that Aponi had left on his neck. After a while, the pain had subsided and Catori just felt a numbness all throughout his body. His eyes had been closed so all he was able to hear was the monster tearing away at his flesh until he could no longer hear anything at all. The numbness along with a lingering silence confused him. It was like the eye of the storm. Calm and quiet, but you were sure horror would come next. He waited. And waited. For something... he didn't want to open his eyes, afraid of being face to face with the monster again. For some reason, he no longer felt the weight upon him that had once been there. Through great reluctance, he peeked one eye open. Then, both. He was back at the pond again with Aponi. It was like he was living in a dream...a dream where he would never have to see her hurt again. She turned and waved to him as he walked into the light and sat beside her.

Full Circle

24

"Take Aponi back to the longhouse. They will care for her wounds there," Annowan handed Aponi over to one of the men that stood beside him. His son had just run off to go deal with the Wendigo on his own. This is everything he tried to prevent. His worst nightmare had come true.

"We will come with you, Annowan." The other men said. They would give their lives for the tribe. But he knew that they needed good men to get them through the remainder of the winter.

"I will handle this. You go back and make sure everyone is ok," he called back and continued on around the outside of the island. He could hear the beast's growls.

When Annowan got there, it looked like it was too late. Catori was nowhere to be found. In a pool of blood, there lay someone that he had not seen for many... many winters... longer than his son, Catori, had even been alive. His brother, Abornazine was there. He ran over to his side and touched his fingertips to his neck. He felt a faint beat on his fingertips.

"Abornazine, you are alive." He said, not knowing what else to say. He knelt beside him, not caring that his legs would be covered by the pool of blood that surrounded. His brother lay there, tears streaming down his cheeks.

Annowan put his arms around his brother's back and held him up to his chest in a hug, but he just continued to sob endlessly. He pulled away.

"I couldn't stop it. I couldn't save him. Your son," he said. Abornazine's lips trembled as he looked past Annowan's shoulder.

"There's nothing we can do now," Abornazine whispered. He got up as fast as he could and Annowan followed suit. Abornazine continued to look past where Annowan stood, so he followed his gaze to see the Wendigo that had once taken over his brother. It began running towards them, but a radiant light beamed from behind the Wendigo. It came around towards the front and Annowan could see the buck that had warned him that day that he found he was going to be a father. That day many, many winters ago.

"We need to run. This is what Catori gave his life for. So that we could be safe," Abornazine said.

"Then I need to give my own so that he can have his back," he said.

"No. He just feasted. It is only here to kill, now." Abornazine grabbed Annowan's hand and they began to run. Annowan looked over his shoulder and could see the buck trying to hold the Wendigo off. Suddenly, he had forgotten where he was even going and where the entrance to the island was. A glistening owl appeared and led them the remainder of the way. When he looked at that owl, all he could think of was his father for some reason. He laid his trust in it.

When they reached the entrance of the island, they could see that the pathway that led there from the mainland was washing up. They ran as fast as they could, careful not to get carried away with the currents. About halfway down the path, the water came up to their knees but both of the brothers continued on. They had finally made it to the mainland and knew they were safe. Both of them looked out as the pathway was almost completely concealed by the waters and there was no way to go there until the next low tide.

What once had been his son, was now a monstrous creature that would lurk the cursed island until the spirit of the Wendigo found another soul to feast on...

Epilogue

The Paugussett Tribe lived on the shoreline of what is now known as Connecticut. Their land extended from New Haven down to the Westport area. This tribe flourished on the availability of fish, shellfish and wildlife from the coast. Due to low tide, more food such as crabs and clams would be uncovered and help them survive through the difficult winters. The springs and water were especially sacred to this tribe as it meant life everlasting. As the Europeans came into their territory in the 17th century, deadly diseases such as smallpox were transmitted to them. At first, the Europeans worked with the Paugussett tribe for trade as they used their wampum to purchase fur from Albany, New York. The Paugussett Tribe was peaceful in the way that they tried to coexist along the Europeans all while maintaining their rituals and customs.

Unfortunately, the Europeans eventually took their land and forced what remained of the Paugussetts into starvation or freedom by running away. Some reservations were set up in the past, but additional land was continuously taken from them until none remained. Forced into assimilation, the Native Americans were able to become American citizens in the 1900's and eventually were allowed to automatically gain citizenship through birth in America.

For more information about the Paugussett Tribe, please read:

"A History of Connecticut's Golden Hill Paugussett Tribe"

by Charles Brilvitch

Charles Island Disclosure

Charles Island is located in Milford, Connecticut and is a state park. The sandbar (tombolo) between Silver Sands State Park and Charles Island over washes twice daily with tidal flooding which produces dangerous currents and undertow. No one should walk on any portion of the tombolo when it is covered with water.

Attention Hikers!

It is important to know walking all the way to Charles Island is not always possible. Low tides do not always uncover the tombolo completely. See Milford Harbor/Connecticut tide chart for tide details.

NO CROSSING May 1st to September 9th due to natural area preserve for nesting birds!

Acknowledgements

Thank you Charles Brilvitch and the Bridgeport Public Library for supplying me with a plethora of information to describe The Paugussett Tribe's customs and way of living

I am grateful for the Maryland Writing Association for providing countless workshops and networking opportunities to learn more about publishing and writing.

Finally, thank you to my family and friends for supporting me on my writing journey and always cheering me on and providing feedback. I couldn't do it without you!

Catori's story continues...

Winter 2022

Turn the page for a sneak peek of
Captain Kidd's curse in another Tale of
Charles Island:

The Cursed Vessel

COMING JUNE 2022

The Dream

1

Steady seas made for the perfect day of sailing or

boating. Persistent swishing of the waves as they gently

came in against the sandy shores, they carried multiple

shells back to sea with them again and again. When the

sun peeked out of the puffy white clouds, it urged me all

the more to be out there. I longed to be with the

shipmates, even starting out with the worst job of

scrubbing the deck floor or cooking for hours on end for

the entire crew. I could hear the floorboards creak as I

walked down the deck, introducing myself to the captains who would likely care less. Seagulls swarming the skies, letting out a screech for their own friend had taken their catch for the day. This reminded me much of humans for many would take credit for the other's work or steal their earnings and keep them as their own. This was all a dream of mine though. I would find myself up on this hill, peering out at the ships - thinking of how different my life would be if I had the life of a crewmate. But that was just the first step. My desire to someday be captain was the true endpoint that I aimed for most. There was something about letting the wind guide your sail to and fro. A natural sense of curiosity came just from the very idea of one day having a ship of my own. A crew of my own. To voyage anywhere I wanted at any given time and have that freedom.

Each and every day, I would wake up and sneak out of my house to run up the hill to watch the sunrise. Smooth blurs of orange crept over the horizons, illuminating it in an ethereal glow as if the very edge of earth was on fire. Instead, everything in this glow's path radiated in warmth and light. In the small town of Greenock, a picturesque landscape of mountains and valleys made up the surrounding territories aside from the lone village. Port Glasgow thrived with imports and exports - colossal ships came and went each and every day. It seemed that everyone was in a constant state of bustling around this way and that. Even from the roads, you could see the ships' masts poking over roofs of houses along the way. As I climbed up the small hill near my home to watch that sunrise, I remember watching the ships in awe and utter admiration for its crew. As soon as the sun came into full view from the horizons, I jumbled back down the hill to get back home before it was noticed that I snuck out. Peering down the roads, I could see father in the top floor's window, extending both his arms up and out for a nice morning stretch. At that point, I stopped - backing up against the cold, brick wall that belonged to a building adjacent, as to not be caught out. Peering around the corner of where I had just stood, I saw that father was no longer in the window and I ran towards the back of the house. That gave me just a few moments before he would be downstairs and looking for me. Beside our house, our neighbors always kept various types of flowers. Tall stalks of thistle shot out from the ground and leaned towards the sun that had just made its appearance in the sky. Contrasting to the towering stalks were delicate bluebells, which were also purple despite their name, but delicately poked out of the dew-covered grasses. Mother resembled the bluebells most. She would wake every morning before father and scurry downstairs to set a proper table with the meager portions of food that we were able to afford as a family. I did not resemble her in the slightest if not for the light green eyes that passed down to me. I grabbed a bunch of bluebells and headed up the back steps. Mother was in on my secret as long as I didn't get caught from father. I tried my best to sneak inside through the back door, but the creaking steps announced my presence. Before I could grasp the handle of the door in my fingers, it swung open and father stood in the doorway, eyebrows furrowed down.

"Boy, you must not venture out there without us knowing. We've told you that time and time again," I looked over at mother and saw her sympathetic face as she too must have had a dream similar to mine. But the difference with me, was that I was not going to let anything come in the way of that dream. Father must have noticed my gaze as I looked over at her instead of him and he too looked back at mother who broke her eye contact from me and continued cleaning after breakfast.

"Don't think she's going to help you, if you're going to be the man of this family you've got to straighten up," he said, rigidly.

The man of the family. What a joke. That didn't seem to work very well for him. He followed everything that he was supposed to do and listened to his superiors except we still were left with scraps of food each night despite all of his struggles each day. I would be the man of the family, but I would actually come through.

About the Author

Marissa is the author of a memoir and the Tales of Charles Island series. Marissa mostly writes fictional stories and began by journaling and writing screenplays in elementary school for her peers to perform. She spends much of her time with her pets aside from traveling to new places and journaling.

Born and raised in Connecticut, she holds New England close to her heart and many of her stories are based in the suburbs of Connecticut.

She has a deep and profound respect for people with special needs as her first job in her field was a special educator. Marissa found her voice through writing. While in high school, she was the editor of the Arts and Entertainment section of the school newspaper. She pursued a degree in Education, minoring in English literature and Anthropology. Later, she went back to school to better understand Autism and graduated with a Master's in Special Education.

Marissa would love to hear from you. Use the links below to connect & hear about upcoming books:

Visit Marissa's Website:
https://marissadangelo.wixsite.com/marissasworldofbooks

Instagram:
https://www.instagram.com/_mysty_writes/

Amazon Page:
https://www.amazon.com/author/marissadangelo

Made in the USA
Middletown, DE
18 May 2022